SILVERADO MIDDLE SCHOOL
C/O JENNIFER LAUER
1133 COOMBSVILLE ROAD
NAPA, CA 94558

The Passage

The Passage

by Norah A. Perez

J. B. Lippincott Company
Philadelphia and New York

U.S. Library of Congress Cataloging in Publication Data

Perez, Norah A
  The passage.

  SUMMARY: Recounts the inhuman conditions en-
dured by a group of Irish emigrants during the ocean
crossing to Canada to escape the famine in 1847.
  [1. Emigration and immigration—Fiction. 2. Ireland
—Emigration and immigration—Fiction] I. Title.
PZ7.P426Pas   [Fic]   74-32278
ISBN-0-397-31616-X

For Megan McCauley

The author is deeply grateful to Edwin C. Guillet, L.L.D., whose magnificent record of the Atlantic crossings by sailing ship from 1770 to 1860, *The Great Migration*, provided the inspiration and much of the source material for this novel.

1

"Name and age?" asked the surgeon. "Are you well? Hold out your tongue. Alright."

And the whole tattered lot of them claimed they were perfectly fit, as spry as Irish grasshoppers. Mr. Roohan, with his windy cough that could blast a sailing ship out of the water. Mrs. Gogarty, so old and gnarled with arthritis that she had to be propped by her elderly husband. Then the Hoult children, thin as spokes, but wearing such robust grins it looked as if they'd all just kicked the landlord. The O'Faoláins next, the tall, bent-shouldered man, his pregnant wife, one popping son, one daughter. And when it was the girl's turn she spoke out, "Cathleen O'Faoláin, sir. Fourteen, and stronger than I look." Stuck out her tongue at him, "Ahhhhhhh."

"Alright," said the surgeon, and passed her. There was nothing to worry about after all. Because in Ireland in 1847 everyone was passed as fit to go to Canada. Except poor, slobbery, muddle-headed Michael McCabe, who only stepped into the line because he felt so lonesome out of it. No, the truth was that in this time of famine Ireland was glad to be rid of them, and as many more of the starving and unemployed as wanted to leave.

The emigrants huddled on the quay in a vast, chill, undulating fog. None of them could see the ocean, but

9

they could taste it on the tingling air, the unimaginable Atlantic. It lay somewhere out there beyond Howth, beyond the Irish Sea, through the North Channel, a great, liquid, shifting bridge to the new land. Bartley O'Faoláin, five years old and brazen with excitement, yelled, "Where's our ship, Cathleen? I want to see it!"

"Do be still for five minutes. It's out there somewhere. Soon the fog will lift."

The child was a windmill, endlessly turning. All was confusion. Hundreds of emigrants crowded along the waterfront, surrounded by their bundles and possessions. They talked, questioned, huddled against a cool May wind. Dogs ran barking among them, sniffing into the provisions, the casks, kegs, kettles, all. There was the endless dreary wail of babies crying. Women shushed, rocked, fed them.

Holding Bartley's rough, small hand, Cathleen was pulled along the quay as they explored the Dublin harbor. It was mysterious, fascinating. The strange geometry of tall-masted sailing ships tilted here and there through the fog. Glimpses of rigging floated from nowhere into nowhere, torn spiderweb strands. Shouts, cries, hidden laughter. All along the waterfront touters and vendors hustled their wares, emerging from mist to entreat, to demand, to promise, their cupped hands greedy for coins. All had something to show or sell, and contradictory things to tell. Cathleen was excited by their faces, the patchwork clothing, the smells and the noise. She had never experienced anything like it.

She stopped to speak to the Roohans, their neighbors from county Meath. Mr. Roohan sat on a sack, coughing into the wind, while his pillar of a wife rigidly guarded their possessions. A man approached, bundled in a greatcoat. His face was like a clenched fist, hard and aggressive. "What's your ship?"

"Fair Western Lady," said Mr. Roohan.

"She'll probably not sail for a week yet. Maybe ten days."

Severe Mrs. Roohan said, "We were told tomorrow, the eighteenth of May."

The hustler was dirty and sour, with a bright drop hanging from the end of his nose. He wiped it away with his torn sleeve. "She'll sail when she picks up a crew, or when the weather's fit, or when the captain feels like a change of scene, and not before. Now why not come along with me and take lodgings while you wait? You'll get a good hot dinner, and a bellyful of whisky as well."

The woman slammed her arms shut tightly across her chest. "Mr. Roohan has taken the pledge."

"Then I'm sorry for him." The hustler robbed another bright drop from his jeweled nose. "That was foolish, indeed. Did you not know that whisky is the surest thing to prevent the agonies of seasickness? When you're somersaulting on the decks, friend, you'll wished you'd swallowed the prevention in Dublin."

Mr. Roohan looked hopeful. "Are you telling me the truth, now?"

"Any sailor will tell you the same."

Militant, Mrs. Roohan repeated, "He's taken the pledge, promised Father McConaghy, so leave him be."

"If your good priest had ever been seasick himself, then he'd not mind you taking some friendly advice. Medical advice at that. Why do you think they put barrels of the stuff on board for the captain and his crew? You won't see *them* tossing their dinners over the side at the first squall. Steady as timber they'll be, and it's the grog keeps them that way."

"You don't say so!" Bright-eyed, agreeable, Mr. Roohan hopped off the sack. "Then I'll take your word for it."

"Stephen! You'll not go with him."

Cathleen, who had been told to keep a good grip on Bartley, discovered that he'd run off. She pushed her way through the crowds, staring at all the people who waited to board the various ships, who waited to try on new lives in a new country. What a pitiful lot they were, most of them half-starved, dumped like rubbish all along the quay. She thought then of Father McConaghy, blessing their group as they went out of his parish, pouring prayers on their heads like oil upon troubled waters. He was a soft old man, well fed, well housed. Softly he christened them, married them, buried them, but Cathleen knew he'd never burned with hunger, or lost a child; all his griefs were secondhand.

Bartley was out of sight, gone for sure. She would never find him in the fog, and her father would tell her again how careless and irresponsible she was; there would be another row. Mr. O'Faoláin had gone to try to find Captain Greeley of the *Fair Western Lady*. Soon he'd be back with news of when they might expect to sail. But that Bartley, where the devil had he gone? Cathleen hesitated, not knowing which way to look for him. Conversations sparked and flared and died away all along the quay. Slowly the chill, dark face of afternoon turned toward the night.

She had traveled the long, bumpy distance by cart,

been jolted and bruised, held on to bouncing pots and pans. Clutched hold of Bartley, who wriggled and never stopped talking. Slept only a little, eaten hardly at all. Now she was cargo, bound for an unknown country. Soon she would never see Ireland again.

"Cathleen!" It was Bartley, in the baggy trousers, his impudent face crammed under a large, coarse cap. "There's a man wants to sell us a cow! She's a lovely cow, may we have her?"

"Now what would we do with a cow on a ship?"

"Tie a rope on her. Let her swim!"

"We have no money for a cow, Bartley."

"That's alright, then." He grinned up at her. "But I like cows. They've a lovely smell, haven't they?"

2

Morning blew fresh around them. A thinner, paler fog still blanked out the Dublin harbor as all along the waterfront small fires melted warm holes in the numbing mist. All night the emigrants had camped in the open air, afraid to pay the price for lodgings. The emigration pamphlets had warned them not to be cheated of their savings before ever leaving port. But there had been no instructions about how to deal with the cold and delay. They waited, anxious and bewildered, for any news.

Yesterday Liam O'Faoláin had walked along docksides and quays trying to get information about when they might sail. He had talked to ship's agents and emigration officers, and they had all referred him back to the mysterious Captain Greeley. Nobody knew the present whereabouts of the man. Someone said he'd died of cholera, and another was certain he'd been shipwrecked off the Azores.

Mr. O'Faoláin was concerned. As spokesman for his neighbors from county Meath, he had bargained, amid all the clamor and competition of the ship's brokers, for their passage as a group, and had finally obtained a cheaper steerage rate for "the whole as a lump."

"And no wonder the rate was so favorable," he said to his wife. "It appears we've contracted passage on a ghost ship, commanded by an invisible captain, and manned by a spiritual crew."

Cathleen laughed. Her father's black eyebrows shut together as a signal he had not intended to be amusing.

Mr. Roohan, patrolled by his wife, came by to boast of the good dinner and the fine, warm bed he had enjoyed in his lodging house nearby. Mrs. Roohan contradicted every word he said.

"Crammed in like herring in a keg, we were, with the worst riffraff I've ever set eyes on. Trampled by bedbugs! Eaten by lice! Why, I've fed better scraps to my own pigs than I've been served up in that terrible place. And Mr. Roohan, soggy with drink since we arrived."

"A friendly nip . . ." Mr. Roohan sidled up to Mrs. O'Faoláin and offered her his jug. "As a precaution against the seasickness."

She only laughed, and gave him a nudge with her elbow. "I can see you've absorbed enough of that stuff to see you safely across the Atlantic and the seven seas as well, Mr. Roohan. But thank you, no."

None of it bothered Cathleen, not the dampness, nor the discomfort, nor the delay. She had spent fourteen parched years, dependent on a potato patch for life itself. If the plants flourished, that meant another year of survival. If they blackened and withered, then that meant illness, starvation, or death, or, even worse than that in her father's opinion, the parish relief. During the blight a sister had died, burned out with fever. Cathleen was glad to be gone from such misery. Nothing could be more exhilarating than the Dublin scene.

She and Bartley followed their father about the waterfront, stopping along the way to read the advertisements pasted up in warehouses and brokerage firms, announcing the speed and comfort of dozens of sailing ships, and their dates of departure. Yet nobody could believe much of what they saw, and even less of what they heard. Tales were told of vessels that delayed for days, with sails unbent and no sign of a crew. Then, with the sudden flutter of a rising bird, they were gone, bewildered passengers left behind, snatching up babies, bedding, old butterkeg water casks, shrieking for watermen to help catch the runaway ships.

Vendors approached, offering gingerbread, tinware and tools, cheese, boots, useful things, useless things.

"I want it!" Cows or crockery, Bartley wanted it all. Cathleen dragged him past the temptations. One of her mother's favorite expressions was "The squeaky wheel gets the grease." And Bartley, once the squeakiest wheel in county Meath, was bound and determined to roll up a similar reputation on the Dublin waterfront.

"I swear you were born greedy," she told him. Yet he amused her just the same. From the minute his eyes sprang open in the morning until sleep slammed them shut at night, Bartley pounced on every day and shook it out for all it was worth. Cathleen, her mother said, had been the very same, and still was.

"Hssst." It was an old lady, layered in strange rags. One of her eyes was sunk shut under a monstrous growth, and the other obscenely winked. "What'll you have, darling? Nuts, sweets, oranges? The little boy wants an orange, don't you, love?"

"Yes, I do!"

"And ribbons . . . See, here they are, and look at all my pretty laces."

Cathleen stared. Objects were brought up from the depths of a bulging bag, tantalizingly flashed, plunged down again. She was afraid that her father, who stood talking to a seaman only steps away, would see her dealing with a vendor.

"Everyone has a little money." The old woman winked her sound eye open and shut, open and shut.

Bartley broadcast, "Cathleen has sixpence, she does. Aunt Wig gave it to her. I swallowed mine."

"Sixpence to see your own sweet smile," hissed the woman, and up out of her bundle flashed a little pocket mirror. Cathleen's face danced in it.

"Buy it, Cathleen. Give her your money." Bartley yanked at her shawl.

She fumbled for the hidden money and quickly paid for the mirror, tucking it out of sight. She knew that her father would disapprove, because he disapproved of almost everything she did. But she had this curiosity about herself, the mysterious landscape of her own person, seen only from the inside looking out. Who was she? What was she really like? To her father something faulty, someone to be changed. And once she had heard her mother tell Aunt Wig, "Cathleen has a good heart and a good quick mind and the face of a holy saint, but, oh, the folly of that lashing tongue. When the girl speaks out they must hear her in Wales."

Aunt Wig laughed, and said she wished they could hear her in London, where it might do some good among the English politicians. Aunt Wig, nicknamed for her wiry, wrinkled bunch of metallic hair, was married to a shopkeeper in Limerick, and she had given to Cathleen the image of herself she wanted to believe. "You were born backside first," Aunt Wig had said, "and maybe that's why you've always looked at things in a different way. But there's nothing wrong with that, nor with you, love. You've never been afraid of the truth. Some people are, you know."

Sailors elbowed them aside, as they shoved along the crowded waterfront. Cathleen watched them, fascinated. Exotics they were, their faces shaped and colored in a dozen foreign countries. Shouting, laughing, swearing, they rocked past the staring emigrants in their loose trousers and pilot jackets, round hats with streamers set back on their heads. Soon the Irish would trust their lives to this wild, rackety bunch. Some of them were not much older than Cathleen, but boys who had wrestled with rope and sail and weather seasoned early into men. One of them accidentally bumped against her, knocking her off balance. She was set back on her feet. A smile, a wink, a "Sorry, miss," and he was gone in the fog.

Mr. O'Faoláin returned, the anxiety in his face smoothed away.

"Did you learn anything, Father?"

"I had words with the first mate of our brig. It's firm, then. We sail tomorrow."

The mist was lifting. Faint, cold sunshine stroked the harbor, coaxing into full outline a reality of merchant vessels, barques and brigs, steamers and tugs, fishing boats and dories. The water was filthy, full of floating garbage.

"But where's our ship? I want to see it now!" Bartley threw his cap up into the air.

Cathleen glanced along the harbor, hoping that she would be the first to catch sight of the *Fair Western Lady*, its sails sketched white as gulls' wings on the brightening sky. Instead, she saw only a welter of masts, ropes, ladders, yardarms, clusters of sailing ships still naked without their flapping canvas shirts.

3

The nineteenth of May, 1847. A day cold, bright, glazed with an icy wind. Liam O'Faoláin had found at last their brig. Boarded her, stored some of their provisions, spoken for a berth. Then he was gone to the customhouse to clear through the rest of the baggage. Forty emigrants had traveled together from Father McConaghy's parish, and forty-strong they intended to stay. There was only the final step now of setting sail together.

All the time they had shivered at the harbor, the *Fair Western Lady* had been anchored nearby, sleeved in the fog. Ever since she had first heard its name the brig had floated, in Cathleen's imagination, as flawless as a ship's model sealed within glass. But as they rowed toward it in the dory, she saw a clumsy, square-cut bow and stern. The brig squatted low on the water, with no grace or precision at all. Even the figurehead was a disappointment. It had been hacked from a massive block of pine, and the body of the lady herself, set solidly below the bowsprit, was homely and stout. She stared out to sea, one hand clumsily shading her squint. Her bodice was lacquered black, and cut so tight and low that her bumpy wooden breasts toppled over. The skirt was red, curving high over a fat rump. She was awkward and common, a regular eyesore.

Mrs. O'Faoláin went carefully up the rope ladder, followed by two of the skinny Hoult children. Bartley was next, and as he set his heels on the deck he said to the sailor who had offered a hand, "Is this our ship to go across the sea on? She's a rotten old tub, isn't she?"

The young sailor laughed, and reached out to help Cathleen. "We'd better straighten out a few things, lad. This is a brig, do you see? A ship has three masts, and we've only two. And while she may be an old tub, and as creaky in her joints as your own granny, she's *not* rotten. And she'll see the likes of you safe across the Atlantic."

"I like your hat! May I try it on?"

Cathleen said, "Pay no attention to him, please. That Bartley's as bold as a cat's claw."

The sailor set her down on deck. "Oh, I'd give him my hat if I had one to spare." He took it off his head and set it on top of Bartley's wild hair. "When we get to the new land you may have it to keep, and that's a promise." When he smiled again, and winked at her, Cathleen recognized him as the sailor who had bumped her off balance the day before. This time his delighted stare went on for so long that poor Mrs. Hoult, as fat as her children were thin, and puffing hard from her climb up the ship's ladder, had to gasp out for his help.

The deck seethed with emigrants. They stumbled over crates and cordage, gaped up at foremast and mainmast, crowded around the forecastle at the bow, where the sailors berthed. Bumping, jostling, interested, awed, they examined the ship's great wheel, the wooden case called the binnacle, which housed a compass and a light, the apparatus used to weigh anchor and hoist the sails. Children teased the chickens in their coop under the longboat. The hatches stood open, and the Irish flowed up and down the ladders that led between decks.

Mrs. O'Faoláin, who was eight-months pregnant, tired easily. "I think I'll go down and find our berth, Cathleen. I'm that wrung out from all this confusion."

"Not me." Bartley stepped backward from the fore-hatch. "I don't want to live down in that hole."

"Come along now, no fuss. It can't be that bad."

The only light in the humid tunnel below filtered down through the open hatchways. Two rows of double bunks ran the length of the steerage, each berth about five feet long and ten feet wide. In the center aisle, between the tiers, was a narrow space where baggage and provisions were to be stored. Already it was crammed with an assortment of chests, clothing, and utensils. The steerage was just high enough for Cathleen to stand upright, and she was barely five feet tall. "Och, the poor men," she said, as they groped their way along in semidarkness. "After a few weeks of this they'll be permanently bent."

"Ah, here's our own." Mrs. O'Faoláin sighed, and sat down on a lower berth. Stacked in front, in the congested corridor, was their supply chest, with its new padlock, and their other goods, locked up or tightly lashed with twine.

"Why can't we sleep up there?" Bartley pointed to the upper compartment, where the Hoult family had taken possession. Young Johnny hung by his heels, staring at them upside down. His brothers and sisters overflowed from above, in a dangling assortment of arms, legs, heads, grins.

Mrs. Hoult, still out of breath, paused wheezily at the

ladder. "Dear knows," she said, "I expected to sail the Atlantic, not climb it."

A small, determined woman suddenly appeared, her mouth twisted up into a hard pinch, elbows cocked on her hips. "Here now," she said to the O'Faoláins, "you've stolen our berth. You can get out, the whole dirty lot of you."

"Indeed, we have not. My husband picked out this place early in the morning, and our straw mattress is here already, marked with our name as clear as daylight." Mrs. O'Faoláin stayed where she was, using Bartley as an anchor. "You can see that we're settled."

"Well, you can just *unsettle.*" The woman snatched up a litter of listless children and set them in an untidy row on the berth. "Now, I say this is ours, and you can take your mattress and go somewhere else."

All along the packed aisle there were other arguments and scuffles. Children screamed and wailed, women pushed and shoved in a scramble to find the best places. Shouts, cries, angry insults. Boxes were dragged backward and forward. From some far-off place came the sad complaint of a violin.

"We'll not budge."

"*I* say you will!"

"You leave us alone," said Cathleen.

"And who asked you to interfere, Miss Impudence?" The pinch-faced woman gave her a shove.

"I'm going to fetch the captain," Cathleen told her mother. "He'll settle this row soon enough."

The woman stared fiercely, hesitated, and then, without another word, picked up her children and shoved them back into the shadowy depths of the steerage. All around was a brawling confusion as the emigrants sorted out their belongings and began to set up housekeeping. Two or three sailors moved around in the disorder, directing single men to the stern, single women to the bow, and families to the area between. Everyone shouted questions at them. What about water rations and cooking privileges? Where were the water closets?

Cathleen felt as if invisible hands had grabbed her by the throat and were squeezing all the air out of her lungs.

"I wonder if we've done the right thing," said Mrs. O'Faoláin, still holding on to Bartley.

"Right or wrong," Cathleen told her, "it was the only thing left to do."

4

A fine holiday mood tickled the crowd that stretched out along the waterfront. The *Fair Western Lady* was due to sail at any minute. Sailors ran up the shrouds and lay along the yardarms. The anchor was hoisted, the topsails unreefed, and a few passengers still on the quay shouted for the captain to wait for them. Packages were tossed. A crate of chickens that was being lifted over the side dropped back into the dirty water and floated away in a squawk of feathers.

On the dock relatives and friends, or idle strangers with nothing better to do, waved their hats and shouted their farewells. Scarves and ribbons streaked gay colors on the wind.

"You'll all be gentlemen!"

"Look up Mick Flaherty in Prescott."

"When you're rich, be sure and send for me."

Songs and laughter splashed out from noisy dockside taverns, where glasses clinked a parting toast.

Slowly the brig moved out into the rumpled bay.

"Stop this boat!" It was Mrs. Roohan, who had been anxiously patrolling the foredeck. "Mr. Roohan has been left behind!"

"There he is!" Cathleen pointed him out, as his uncertain feet scribbled him along through the crush of spectators. Friendly hands slapped him on the back, gave him a boost and a final heave in the direction of a waterman just pulling away. Mr. Roohan's leap was theatrical, and the splash that followed quite spectacular. On deck, Mrs. Roohan shrieked for Saint Christopher, while the grinning waterman, who had rescued a drowning bonnet and the crate of hysterical chickens, pulled Mr. Roohan out of the bay. Oars chopping fiercely, he followed along in the wake of the brig while Mr. Roohan coughed himself sober in the bottom of the dory.

A bright sense of freedom floated among the passengers on deck. Children ran about, crawled under the longboat, and dangled from the rigging. Adults introduced themselves to strangers, smiling into the sunshine. The women were polite and sociable, laughing as they exchanged bits and pieces of information. A list of rules and regulations was nailed to the foremast, but nobody was yet much interested in details. It was a time of celebration and release.

Tobacco juice rained down upon the deck. The ship's surgeon produced a fiddle, and as he scraped up the familiar shape of an Irish jig, a well-built girl of twenty immediately pulled up her skirts and set her feet flashing into the dance. Young men and old formed a circle around her, rough hands clapping, feet stamping out the rhythm. Gulls wheeled upon the blazing blueness overhead. The girl had strong arms and vigorous, broad hips. As her coarse skirts lifted and swung, her eyes, lips, and teeth glistened, and her polished hair spilled loose into the breeze.

"Go on, Cathleen, you can do it," Bartley shouted.

She was excited by the lighthearted mood of the music.

Her feet suddenly started to move and flung her into the jig. Her skirts swirled wildly in the air. She laughed. Tilting back her head, she saw, high in the rigging, the smiling face of the young sailor who had helped her on board that morning. She turned lightly this way and that as the men shouted and stamped to the music.

"By the powers, them two will stir enough wind to drive us out of the channel."

"This trip will be no punishment if we've entertainment as fine as this."

Cathleen was seized, half dragged and half carried, and set down with a sudden thump on a cask. Her father's face, black-browed, furious. "Do you dare to make an indecent exhibition of yourself!"

"What have I done?"

"Jigging about like a brainless puppet, showing off your legs like a street arab! Whatever were you thinking of?"

She flashed back, "There's no harm in it!"

"I say there is, making yourself a public display!"

A sparkling tension flared between them. "I was dancing, that's all. And there's nothing wrong with that."

"You can go and stay below, until I've time to deal with you."

"I won't miss our leave-taking. I have a right to see Ireland for the last time, I do!"

"You have no rights but those I give you, and I tell you now to go below."

Bartley ran up, pulled on his father's sleeve. "They're wanting us for roll call, and Mother says to come."

Sailors moved among the passengers, directing them

toward the area of the forecastle, where they would have to pass muster. "Have your tickets ready, and please answer when your name is called."

"We'll discuss this later, Cathleen."

She managed to get the final word. "I did nothing wrong."

The passenger broker's clerk had come on board and now stood ready to take account of them. He was a short man, fattened with importance, and he held a long list ready in his hand. The ship's surgeon put aside his fiddle and came to make sure no helpless or deformed had slipped past the official medical examiner. He was a frail, pale stick with strangely staring eyes, who looked as if he needed a dose of something bitter and strong just to keep him awake.

The clerk's great ringing gong of a voice: "Patrick Bowen?"

"Here, sir."

"Is your wife goin'?"

The clerk grinned. He thought of the deck as his stage and of himself as a performer and a great wit. Each time he chimed out an emigrant's name, he pinned a rhyme to it.

"She is, sir, and our three children. One under twelve for half-fare, and two under seven for one-third."

"Ah, yes. Thank you, Mr. Bowen." The clerk made a check mark on his list, rotating slowly on his heels. He enjoyed the fresh breeze, the showery May sunshine, and the idea that soon all of these wretched people would be a burden somewhere else. As long as so many were willing and anxious to book passage, then his job was secure and his own family fed.

"Jimmy Bryce?" Wagging a playful finger. "Half-fare for lice."

There was some embarrassed laughter and whispered comments among the Irish.

James Bryce stepped forward. Unsmiling, he replied with dignity, "I have no lice, sir."

"Sheamus and Molly and Katie Congreve, you must show me your tickets before you may leave."

Nobody laughed this time, except the clerk. The surgeon passed his dazed eyes over the three in a brief inspection and pronounced them all fit.

There was some commotion in the steerage. Sailors, with long sharp sticks, poked and prodded into all the berths, barrels, and baggage to prick out any stowaways, but none could be found.

Cathleen walked toward the stern, where she could be away from her father and out of his sight. She was still flushed with the humiliation of being scolded like a child in front of everyone, and for nothing at all. She knew Liam O'Faoláin was a difficult man, a man who was often wrong about many things, but to treat her as something disgusting and shameful, as a public disgrace! Her mother had told her many times that her father's life had been too hard, it had often warped his judgment, made him silent, suspicious, and sad. He trusted only his wife, and liked nobody else. No, Bartley could sometimes make him smile, but never Cathleen. He seemed to hold a secret resentment against her, as if it angered him that she could enjoy life so much and he so little. Bartley he would sometimes hold, but he never touched Cathleen. This coldness was a sorrow, and it left her eager for affection, grateful to anyone who offered any. Yet there was so much in him that she did admire. Strength, honesty, independence—these were fine things. Why couldn't he discover something in her to admire? Even when she was a little girl he'd called her forward, rebellious, unmanageable when she had only wanted to be noticed.

A boy of about sixteen stood staring out across the water as they rounded the promontory of Howth.

"Do you hate to leave Ireland so much?" Cathleen said.

"Hate to leave? Why should I? I'm glad to go. It was stay and starve."

"What's your name?"

"Timothy Healy."

"Well, Tim, if you're so glad to go, then why are you so black in the face about it?"

He frowned at her, thinking it over. "It's what lies ahead. I've been wondering how it would feel to be buried at sea."

"I don't imagine, once you're dead, it really matters much where you're buried."

"Oh, but the sea is such a dreadful place." His voice was low, dreary, toneless. "Full of those terrible sharks, and slimy blobs of jelly that can suck you up, and sea monsters, too."

"Sea monsters? Oh, that's foolish."

"Yes, there are monsters! I've seen pictures in books. Like serpents, they are—except fifty times bigger, with bumps on their backs as big as barrels. I wouldn't like to be buried at sea."

"It's not likely you will be."

"Then, of course," he went on, eyes pasted wide and unblinking on his white face, "I do worry about the possibility of shipwreck. Happens all the time, you know, especially near Newfoundland, where it's foggy. Rocks there, like terrible knives that slash up out of the sea and . . ." He made a violent slicing gesture with his hands, and a horrible ripping sound through his teeth. ". . . poke holes out of the bottoms of ships. Happens very regular."

"This breeze ought to give us a fine start, don't you think?"

"And then—there's always the worry of ship fever. Now that's a fearsome thing. People's heads blow up as big as baskets and then burst. Black spots crawl spiderlike all over their bodies, and then there's this *terrible* stink. Or cholera, that's *worse*."

Timothy Healy's clothing, Cathleen noticed, was made from some awful dark stuff, the sort of sacking kittens were drowned in.

"Well, Tim, I must be going."

"And icebergs, too, to be reckoned with. Sure, they look so pure and white—and innocent as wedding cake. But they can gnaw a ship to splinters in an instant. Horrid shrieks. Icy water. Drowning. Gone."

Bartley again. Bowling himself along the deck, knocking people aside like skittles. "Cathleen, Father says you have to come for roll call."

The gloomy boy warned him, "Mind you don't topple overboard, the way you're careening about. One lurch of the ship. Giant wave. Plop. Gone for good."

Soon the broker's clerk was into the *O*'s.

"Liam O'Faoláin? How many are sailin'?"

31

5

They were nearing the end of the alphabet. Mrs. Russell was told to hustle.

"Here I am."

It was the pinch-faced woman who had tried to take the O'Faoláins' berth, along with her tribe of weary children. Instead of five there were only four, and Mrs. Russell held something large and heavy under her shawl.

"Four children under seven, am I right?"

"That's right." Voice tight, flinty. "And the infant in arms goes free."

The clerk glanced at the shawl, at the lively motion within it. He grinned at the surgeon, spun on his heels. "That appears to be a fine, large baby, Mrs. Russell."

She stared at him, hard in the face. "Twelve pounds at birth and gaining every minute, the little devil."

"And how old is this phenomenal infant?"

"He'll be two years this twenty-third of June."

There was more stifled motion as Mrs. Russell held on to the baby with a threatening squeeze. A small, stuffed voice gasped out from under the shawl, "You're choking me, Ma."

"A large baby," said the clerk, "and a proper genius to talk so plain at such an early age." He probed the shawl with his forefinger and then jerked it back. "Why, the little bastard bit me!"

The "infant in arms" was dumped upon the deck. He was a shriveled boy of eight or nine, with a swollen, purple face. "You almost choked me," he screamed at his mother.

"Half-fare," clanged the clerk.

"Don't have it."

"Half-fare, or back he goes to Dublin with us."

"Take him."

"Ma!" The boy began to cry, pulling at her hands. "Don't give me away."

She raged, "A helpless widow-woman, going to a frozen land full of snow and wild animals and savages, and all of you heartless brutes. Well, I don't have the money for him, so you'll just have to take him and leave him to starve in the Dublin streets. There's nothing I can do about it."

"Here now, we'll have none of this." Mr. Roohan pulled off his cap and threw some coins in it. "Nobody's going to let any such thing happen to the poor little chap, so just put in what you can manage, and we'll make up the fare." The cap was passed from hand to hand until the clerk was satisfied. Mrs. Russell gave the boy a slap on the ear for being discovered, and thanked nobody for his generosity.

Fires glared on either side of the foredeck. The women stood in long lines, in caps and shawls, holding on to frying pans, pots, and kettles as they waited a turn at the grates. The breeze had blown up, salt and strong, and they pulled their plaid shawls tightly around their bodies. Children, hopping now with hunger, still played on deck, but their laughter was softer, tugged off by the wind.

The fires burned in large wooden cases lined with bricks. Iron bars set in front contained the living coals. As they waited, the women chatted and joked; a holiday courtesy kept them easy and thoughtful with each other. Those already at the grates hurried so that others could have their turns. They had been told that cooking must be finished by seven o'clock. Overhead, sailors loosened sails, bracing the yards around to catch the wind. They were now off Carlingford, with the mountains of Mourne in sight.

Mrs. O'Faoláin moved forward slowly and clumsily, without her usual vitality.

"Feeling alright, Mother?"

"A bit tired. After all, it's been such a day. Have you seen Bartley?"

"Oh, he's forever fooling about at the water closets. He and Johnny Hoult are just fascinated by *that* arrangement."

"I'm not so fascinated myself." Mrs. O'Faoláin was very shy. "That terrible place below for the women. I'll never get used to the lack of privacy."

She was a little, light woman but now she seemed to be one ballooning belly. Cathleen thought her face was beautiful. Strong cheekbones, chin marked with a wide cleft, deep-set eyes of a wildflower blue. And Moira O'Faoláin had wonderful hair. Not like Aunt Wig's, a family joke, but thick, wavy, full of autumn lights. Except now, Cathleen noticed for the first time, there were touches of white here and there, like frost on morning grass.

"We'll never see Wig again," her mother said.

"Oh, but we will. Of course we will."

34

"No, Cathleen. Everything I've loved is buried to me now."

Cathleen knew that she meant sister, child, homeland, but the words stung just the same.

"Not everything. Not us, not me. I'm with you."

Her mother, embarrassed by sentiment, said nothing at all. Cathleen wanted to touch her, but felt awkward, unable to comfort anyone. She was the oldest, the only daughter left, and yet her parents thought of her as a careless child. All the tension and excitement of the day suddenly drained away. Cathleen stood in silence, waiting for their turn at the fire grate.

An argument flamed at the galley. Many of the emigrants had contracted to have their food supplied by the ship and had paid in advance for the privilege. Now they confronted the black cook, nicknamed Doctor Jones, demanding rations. He stood with his arms knotted across his chest, stubbornly shaking his head from side to side. Beside him the rough-tongued first mate backed his refusal to serve out any meals until the following day.

"There'll be beef and bread in the morning, but Doctor Jones here, he's not well enough to feed the mob of you tonight."

The cook's face was a mass of wrinkles and scars. A piece of red rag, tied tightly around his temples, looked like a bloody scar. One of his ears was slashed off, two fingers from one hand were gone, and the thumb from the other. There wasn't much left of this old piece of gristle, but what there was was stringy and determined. Tonight they could starve as far as he was concerned. Unless . . .

The first mate grinned. Rum? Well, yes, some rum

might sweeten him a little, persuade him to give out the rations. The emigrants argued and complained. One said he would fetch Captain Greeley, but the mate insisted that the captain never got himself involved in silly disputes. The whole thing could be settled smoothly if just this once they bought some grog from the ship's stores to soothe Doctor Jones's bellyache. Finally the rum was paid for, and grudgingly the cook gave out the rations.

Later, Liam O'Faoláin spoke out against the outrage. "We were advised to bring along a gallon of rum as insurance, just to make sure we got our share of water and fair treatment. But it's bribery, plain and simple. I'll go hungry and thirsty before I'll ever consent to such a thing."

Mr. Gogarty asked, "But what else could those folks do?"

"Refuse. Those who paid a bribe tonight will pay it over and over again. You can bet the captain won't interfere if he makes a profit from his rum. And the first mate is probably in for a share. What we have to do is organize ourselves, before things get out of hand. We'll need a committee and a spokesman, right at the outset. Let's think it over tonight, and hope to settle the matter in the morning."

"As far as I'm concerned," said cheerful Mr. Roohan, "we can decide it straightaway. You're the very man, O'Faoláin, to speak for us all and look out for our interests."

The men talked it over, their pipes blinking in the twilight. Some of them were timid; some, like Mr. Gogarty, were very old; others were stupid or simply confused. The captain and crew, the *Fair Western Lady,* the sea itself were mysteries to them. If someone was willing to look out for them they would be agreeable and grateful. In the discussion that went on for nearly an hour, a committee of four was assembled, with Liam O'Faoláin as Head. It was settled.

Cathleen stood and listened. She wanted to join in. She was always interested in any discussion with meat on its bones, in affairs that went beyond household gossip. She was proud of her father and the way the other emigrants listened to his views. He was tough, thorough, and practical, and he had held the family together all through the potato famine. A tenant farmer, he had rebelled against selling his crops of wheat and oats to pay rent to an English landlord while his wife and children went hungry. He had been sickened by the sight of corpses piled high on carts, buried without coffins when the blight was at its worst, and had protested bitterly as neighbors were turned out of their wretched cottages. Thousands had suffered and died, and through it all the British government had looked the other way, unwilling to interfere with an English landowner's right to make a profit from his holdings.

Cathleen would never forget any of it. She and Bartley had spaded the stubble fields, grubbing with their hands for undiseased potato plants. They had seen their three-year-old sister Eileen buried. Sheriffs had razed homes, so that those who had been turned out could never come back, and then the land was cleared so that the English landlords could raise cattle there and turn an even greater profit than before. The O'Faoláins had survived perilous times. Mass protests, government workhouses stormed, a typhus epidemic, spiritual as well as physical desolation. And through it all Cathleen remembered the soft lathery voice of the priest, telling them that they were all sinners, that it was God's will that they should suffer, and that they must submit and pray. It was then that her child's faith had shriveled and died. She had spoken out in anger against the injustice of the British government.

"Why don't they stop collecting rents until this blight is over? There must be no more evictions, or we'll all be murdered. It's only common sense."

"The English aren't going to reform their economic policies by using something as obvious as common sense," said her father. "Even if they do, it will be too late for us. No, I've decided we must emigrate."

"Leave Ireland! But that's what they want us to do. They want to get rid of us all."

"Then we'll oblige."

"We should fight back. We work the land. It's ours more than theirs."

"We've nothing to fight with, Cathleen. There isn't a man left among us with the strength to hurl a pikestaff. Now, I've been reading the emigration pamphlets, and in Canada there's a need for labor and good land is cheap. If I work there as a tradesman for a time we can save for a farm of our own. It's not fantasy. Many have done it already."

"What are you thinking of, Cathleen?"

The shine of a sailor's eyes, in the thick half-light.

"Who told you my name?"

"I asked that fat lady today, when I hauled her in over the side. If she hadn't told me, I'd have dropped her back into the bay." He asked, "Don't you want to know mine?"

"Not particularly."

"Yes, you do. It's Jock Riordan."

"Have you made this crossing before?"

"Many times. I've been three years at sea."

"What will it be like?"

"No two crossings are ever the same. Cholera's bad everywhere this year, so I hope we don't have any of that. Would you like some good advice?"

"I'm not that fond of good advice. It usually means good for somebody else, not for me."

"This is good for both of us. Stay on deck as much as possible. It's healthier here than down below. And that way I'll get a chance to talk to you now and then, when the captain's not looking." He moved along, laughing over his shoulder. "And hang on to your brother's britches when the weather gets rough!"

6

Her father noticed her still on deck and coldly ordered her to go below. As Cathleen went down the ladder into steerage, the first mate followed, a lantern held in one hand. He was burly and squat, and the glow of the light made his features masklike and grotesque. The emigrants were preparing for bed, struggling to open their baggage and find night clothing and settle down the excited children. The mate pushed his way along the center aisle, shouting that all lights must be out by ten o'clock. No lucifer matches were to be used between decks, or unprotected candles, or they could all expect to go up like sparks in the wind. Safety lanterns would burn at the hatchways all night. Fires would be lit on deck at seven in the morning. As he turned to go back up the ladder, he gave Cathleen a hard, fumbling pinch on the thigh.

Liam O'Faoláin had made a tight and compact unit out of their lower berth. He had driven in a line of nails and hung up the clothing and utensils they would need most often during the voyage. In the center aisle he had lashed down the deal chest, with their food supplies locked up inside. It was fashioned like the sea chests used by sailors, with a wide base and sloping sides so that it wouldn't topple or shift in rough weather.

All the children had wanted to sleep in the upper berths. The lucky ones shinnied up and down the supporting posts, laughing and giggling. They climbed in and out, knocked over kettles and kegs, tried out again and again the novelty of the water closets. Men and boys were required to use the facilities on the upper deck, and Mrs. O'Faoláin caught hold of Bartley just as he was about to go up for the third time that evening.

"You'll not make another trip tonight. It's dark and slippery, and you can use the chamber pot instead."

Almost everything they had brought was made of tin: the washbasin, the pots to cook in, a can to drink from, teaspoons, knives and forks, plates and dishes. But Aunt Wig's gift had been brought along for both sentimental and practical reasons. It was a great, china chamber pot, as big as a tureen and decorated with gilt and painted roses.

More and more emigrants poured down the hatchways as the night came on. It was getting rough, and as the brig pitched and rolled, the confusion grew. The men ducked their heads low as they moved slowly up and down the aisle, around the congestion of baggage and supplies. Mr. O'Faoláin, following the advice in the emigration pamphlets, had warned the group from county Meath to take as few possessions as possible, all packed away into small spaces—little objects contained in larger ones, metal and wood instead of china or crockery, and all items clearly identified with the owner's name in case of theft. He'd also suggested that they wear their oldest clothing and most disreputable boots at sea and save their quality garments, if they owned any, for the new land. Feather mattresses had been sold and replaced with cheaper straw, for it was likely these would have to be thrown out at the end of the passage.

It was obvious to Cathleen that some of the other emigrants were not so well prepared. Their luggage was badly packed, their provisions and utensils were already scattered, the berths heaped high with odds and ends, and their children rolled about in the best clothing they owned. Many of them had waited to buy their food supplies in Dublin, and were now complaining about the poor quality and high cost. Mr. O'Faoláin had urged his neighbors to carry along what potatoes they had in strong sacks, to bring turnips and onions, flour, tea, sugar, and whatever else they could scrape together. Some had brought a handful of candles, vinegar and Epsom salts, a chunk of bacon, eggs packed carefully in salt. Others had only some oatmeal and a few dried herring. But everything was tightly wrapped, stoppered, and protected, to prevent any spillage or waste.

Bartley was finally put to bed, laughing as he announced that it was like sleeping on a shelf. Now the brig lurched violently, there was a rising whine of wind, and Mr. O'Faoláin came down from the upper deck to say it looked as if they might be in for a bad night.

Cathleen undressed, realizing what a total lack of privacy there was among a hundred and ten men, women, and children. They were like animals penned in a stable. Already the air smelled of urine and sweat.

It was strange to lie together on the straw mattress, with little room to turn or stretch. Bartley was a roller and a kicker, and the bedding heaved as if a small whale churned under it. Cathleen thought of the Hoult family, with twice as many, packed into the dark space overhead.

Water splashed down the hatchways, and it was decided that they must be closed against the roughening weather. As blackness sealed them in, Cathleen felt as though she had been nailed alive into a coffin.

A dreary cry of babies started up, one after another. Mr. Roohan coughed again and again. There was the croupy bark of a restless child and the sound of a woman crying hysterically. First night at sea.

"Oh, my God." It was a groan from the dark belly of the night. "I'm sick, I'm sick."

Cathleen had been awake for only seconds. She wondered where she was, and why she was being shaken from head to foot. Moans and shouts broke out all around her.

Ship. Night. Storm. A creaking of timbers, a crack of splintering wood, a sudden cry. Shrieking of children, a thud of falling bodies. In the darkness she reached out, grabbed something small and warm. Bartley's voice was in her ear. "Cathleen, I'm scared. Let me out of here."

Her father said, "Hold fast to each other, and no fuss. It's a storm we're into. By and by we'll be out of it again. So just hold fast."

Overhead, in wild fright, the Hoult family sent up a concert of cries and groans. Things fell, bounced, clattered, smashed. There was the awful sound of someone being sick, a fierce smell.

Bartley had wrapped himself all around Cathleen. "Oh, please, let me out."

43

Mrs. O'Faoláin had taken a chill. Her voice rattled, "Hold on, Bartley, the way your father said. We'll be alright."

Children cried harder, louder. The brig was caught in a battle, punched by water, slapped by wind. There were sudden lulls when they could only lie and wait, wondering what would happen next. Then came the crunching impact of water, tearing past the bulwarks, flooding the upper deck, leaking down the hatchways. Over it all was the maddened, high-pitched whistle of the squall. Cathleen imagined the ship's figurehead, hand over eyes, squinting into the storm as she plunged, big-rumped, in and out of the waves.

Bartley sobbed, unable to stop.

"Bartley," she whispered, "don't cry. I'll tell you a tale if you're good. Shush now, it's alright."

"A hole," he wailed. "We're stuck in a big . . . black . . . hole."

"Listen. Remember that nice sailor who helped us on board and promised to give you his hat someday? Jock Riordan's his name, and do you know where he is right now? He's out there, in that gale, probably way up in the rigging, maybe taking in sails or whatever they do when it storms, up where it's cold and slippery and dangerous, and if he makes one wrong move then he's gone. That's a brave thing to do."

"Stupid."

"It's not stupid. It's his job. He has to do it so we'll all be safe and sound come morning."

"Is he wearing his hat?" Bartley was quieter now, and interested.

"Of course he is. And he's like those men at the fair

44

who walk the wires. Except nobody will ever see how courageous he is, or even give him a bit of applause."

"I hope his hat doesn't fall off."

"It won't."

"I'm scared."

"Put your thumb in your mouth, you'll feel better."

"Never mind the thumb," said Mrs. O'Faoláin, still shaking violently. "A Hail Mary will do very well."

Another lull. Overhead a voice shouted orders through a speaking trumpet. Distantly, an answering chant came from the shrouds. Then another smash of water, and a lurching fall.

They were overturned, gone. Cathleen felt cold, and dreadfully sick. Drops of water stung her face. But, no, they were right side up, still afloat. Safe.

"Do you know what Doctor Johnson said about going to sea?" she asked.

"He said a lot of witty things," said her father. "I only hope it was something useful."

"He said it was like being in jail, with the added risk of drowning."

Her father didn't laugh, but her mother did, as she shivered on the lumpy straw mattress, which Bartley had just wet through. Cathleen was pleased. She was tempted to tell another dozen funny things that famous Doctor Johnson had said, but she decided to save them. There would be other storms for sure, if they ever got through this one.

Fragile morning light. Everywhere people sat limply, depressed, staring at the mess. The hatchways were open, and they could all see the total disaster now exposed. The center aisle was ankle deep with water, a ditch full of boots, ruined food, sodden clothing.

"Are we in terrible trouble, Liam?" Pale as dust, Mrs. O'Faoláin lay flat on her back, stricken with seasickness.

He had opened the chests, one by one. "Everything's still tight. Not even an egg smashed, if you can believe it."

"And nothing lost!"

Cathleen laughed. "Only Aunt Wig's chamber pot. It must have floated off."

Her mother asked, "Will you be able to fix breakfast this morning? I don't think I can manage it."

Cathleen's stomach turned over at the thought of food. Jock Riordan had said to stay on deck as much as possible—perhaps fresh air would help. She dressed, shielding herself under the bedcovers. Everything stuck as her fingers fumbled with buttons and hooks. She glanced up. Johnny Hoult watched her, grinning, as he hung upside down from the upper berth.

7

"Prayers?"

"It's the Sabbath," Liam O'Faoláin repeated.

"Prayers!" The captain was incredulous. "On deck? This morning? Are you mad?"

Captain Greeley stood before the small group of men in the rough morning wind, face a thin, gray headstone, a dark grave's length of body. He was drier than sand, than bone, than old cracked leather. His eyes were dark, dead, staring out at them from under his cap. Even his voice lacked life and juice; it creaked like the cranky windlass. "Can't you see that yards and rigging were torn away in the storm? Sails split? A man toppled to his death last night, did you know about that? And you want to clutter up the deck with people saying prayers!"

"There's a small number of us who wish to observe the Sabbath decently, and it's too noisy and congested below. We'll take care to keep out of your way."

"Observe the Sabbath." The captain squeezed the words out between broken teeth. "Observe it in your berths if you will, or in a water closet if you must, but observe it out of my sight!" As Mr. O'Faoláin and the Committee turned away, he shouted after them, "And see that none of you Irish infringe on the afterdeck!"

Cathleen waited in line at one of the fire grates, feeling sicker every minute from the motion of the brig. The

47

wind groaned, and the seas ran high, throwing up the foam sailors called "white sheep." The cliffs of Antrim were visible; soon they would be out of the channel and upon the broad muscular back of the Atlantic. The *Fair Western Lady* rolled heavily with the swells, her decks awash with confusion as exhausted seamen repaired the storm's damage.

Cathleen reached out, touched the arm of a passing sailor.

"I'm glad you're alright, Jock. I heard that a man was lost last night, and I was afraid it might have been you."

His face was raw from strain and lack of sleep. "It couldn't have been me. Cold fear keeps me stitched tight to this old brig in a squall. No, it was a young fellow I only met for the first time yesterday, before we sailed. All excited he was to have signed on. From Connaught, poor lad."

"I thought we were all lost for sure."

"That storm was an infant to some I've been through. Say, what a strange color you are!"

"Riordan!" The first mate gestured roughly. "Get over here and lend a hand."

He was off on the run, but Cathleen would be able to tell Bartley that Jock Riordan had held on to his hat.

The courtesies of the day before had given way to irritation and bad temper as the women waiting in line at the fires tried to keep their footing on the slippery deck.

"Did you know a sailor drowned last night?" It was the girl who had jigged so gaily as they sailed out of Dublin.

Cathleen said she had heard about it.

"I'm sorry for that, but they're a bad lot, all of them. I should think the air would be black-and-blue from the foul language I've been hearing." She was a fresh, good-natured girl with wide sea-green eyes. "I'm Liddy Dillon. Liddy will do. And you?"

"Cathleen O'Faoláin."

"Then your father, he's Head of the Committee, isn't he? I heard some talk of it last night. They say he's the only one allowed to speak for us, or some such rubbish. Well, I'd like to have a few words with that captain and tell him what I think of his crew. Bothering the women before we were out of Dublin Harbor. And that first mate! Nipping and pinching at us—that's one lobster I'd like to throw into a boiling pot."

"Are you traveling alone, Liddy?"

"Yes, alone. And men do pester me, it's always been that way. But never mind, I can take care of myself." Suddenly she laughed. "Cathleen, you're buttoned wrong, all up the front."

"I usually am. My mother says it's because I was born backside first. But today there's a reason. I had to get dressed under the quilt, and with an audience besides."

"The lack of privacy! And me, squeezed in with five others, all tangled up like a pail of squid."

"Where will you be going to in Canada?"

"To Hambleton. My sister's there, with her husband and a heap of children. She says it's a fine, free land with lots of work for those who are willing. Good wages, too. She says I'll sit at table with the master and mistress just the same as kin, nobody thinks anything of it. She can get me a position, and even a husband if I like. But I'd rather choose for myself. She picked a nice man when she married, but he's as ugly as an English politician!"

Liddy shifted her tin pot and her oatmeal, and brought

out a crumpled letter from inside her dress. "I'll read you parts," she said. " 'Dear sister, I hope that you will try your best to get here soon as there is plenty of work to be had at good wages.' Well, I already told you that. Ah! Here she says, 'I am thankful to say that we are situated in a pleasant spot, twelve acres of cleared land, with a house, an outbuilding, a spring, and other fine things. We have also got a cow, a sow with seven pigs, and also chickens, ducks, and geese.' " Liddy turned the page. "She tells me not to be afraid, to trust God and all that sort of thing, and then she says, 'Try to bring your own provisions as all we had was musty beef and biscuit and were sick from it. I was deprived of all my new blankets, stolen out of our berths, a great pity. Even the baby's wee bonnet taken, and shawls and caps. Trust nobody. Here in Canada we all work from sunrise to sunset, but we may rest as often as we like during the day—nobody minds, not like at home. The cholera has been very bad, thousands died. Dear sister, come as soon as you can manage. We'll send what we can for your passage, and find a husband for you here. Your affectionate sister.' " She tucked the letter back into her bodice. "I wish these women would hurry it up, I'm that hungry."

"I'll not be able to swallow a mouthful."

"Well, there's another who feels as badly as you." Liddy pointed to the quarterdeck, an elevated platform at the stern of the ship, which was the territory of the captain and ship's officers. A tall, narrow girl leaned far out over the side, as if she wanted to gulp down all the fresh air she could hold. Her companion did the same.

"Pranced on board yesterday, the two of them," said Liddy. "Her Ladyship's nose stuck up in the air, and that freckle-faced servant girl staggering after, loaded down with books."

"Are they berthed with us?"

"With *us?* No, they're cabin passengers, if you please. With a steward to put a spoon in the lady's mouth and wipe off her chin if she drools."

Captain Greeley, who had stopped to rasp out a command to a Portuguese seaman, spoke to the girl on the quarterdeck.

"Not feeling well, Miss Arnold?"

"I'm quite squeamish this morning, Captain. And I fell in the night and injured my wrist."

"I'll send in the surgeon to have a look at it."

"That would be very kind."

He bowed and passed on. Liddy's smile twitched. "Hurt that little twig of a wrist, did she? Well, I have a lump on my skull that's as big as a fist where a saucepan bounced off it, and bruises elsewhere I don't intend any ship's surgeon to see. I'm colored all over like a foreign flag."

When it was her turn, Cathleen cooked the oatmeal, trying not to look at it or smell it. When she carried it between decks, she found her brother sitting quietly, legs dangling over the bottom of the berth.

"Here, stick something hot behind your ribs." She poured the porridge into a wooden trencher for him.

"I want an orange, Cathleen. The lady has oranges."

Mrs. O'Faoláin said, "I think Bartley has a touch of fever this morning, Cathleen. Will you try to keep him quiet today, and look out for him? I'm so sick I can't raise my head off the pillow."

8

By afternoon few passengers were still attempting to walk on deck. Rough seas broke through the scupper holes, swirled across the gleaming planks, and plunged out the other side. The *Fair Western Lady* creaked in the wind as she dipped in the foam-streaked swells.

Between decks, gripped by seasickness, most of the emigrants lay groaning in their berths. Only the children seemed unaffected; they tumbled about like dice in the center aisle.

Cathleen was left in charge of her mother and brother while Liam O'Faoláin and the Committee talked to the passengers about the ship's rules and asked their cooperation in enforcing them. Everyone would be required to keep the steerage area clean. Men would be recruited as night watchmen to regulate the ventilation. The captain had warned that if rules were broken he would withhold water or rations as punishment. The sick emigrants lay on their backs, heard the words, nodded and moaned, and went on with the business of dying, for that is what they thought they were doing.

Drunken singing came from the quarters where the bachelors were berthed.

"Liddy Dillon!" A rum-thick voice. "Come back here and cheer us up with a jig."

A girl's voice rang out from behind the partition where

the single women were confined. "You sound cheery enough as it is. I'm staying right where I am."

Bartley lay curled on the berth next to his mother. His eyes were strange with fever, and he insisted that he wanted to go to the upper deck and watch the sailors. Cathleen persuaded him to lie quietly while she told him tales, and he wanted to hear the bloodiest ones she knew. When she ran out of those, she remembered what the gloomy boy, Timothy Healy, had said about the sea serpent. Bartley grew excited at the thought of it and wondered if they could catch it with a bit of beef tied to a string. Finally he threw an arm around her waist and fell asleep.

Cathleen listened to the moans, the gagging and complaints, and believed that there was no human misery comparable to the seasickness that rammed its fist down her throat. Her mother dozed, pale and sweating, under the quilt. Cathleen tried to fight the nausea and think of Canada, of a land without landlords, of chickens and ducks and fertile, unbroken soil. Then her stomach twisted inside out, and she thought of nothing but dying, and wished for it soon.

"Where's your brother?"

She had slept. Her father's face bent over her.

"He was here. Beside me."

"Shhhh. Let your mother sleep. Bartley's nowhere about. I've already asked the Hoults, and they haven't seen him, nor has anyone else."

"He must be playing games with the children."

"You were told to mind him, Cathleen. Now we'd better find him before it gets too dark to see."

Light-headed, she sat up. It was rougher than before; the brig bucked, shuddered, lurched back and forth.

"I'll see if he's gone to pester the men at their cards," said her father. "You inquire up front."

Cathleen stumbled over chests, rolling casks, giggling children. "Has anyone seen Bartley O'Faoláin?"

"Who's he?"

"Ain't seen him."

A small arm gestured to the ladder at the hatchway. "Up there."

"Bartley's on deck?"

"He went up a while ago."

In her chest Cathleen felt the first hard knock of fear. It was late in the day. A little light still sifted down through the hatchway, but soon it would be entirely gone. The brig tilted heavily to one side, and water slopped down through the opening, soaking her dress. The rungs of the ladder were slimy. As she set foot on deck a hard wind slapped against her, and the brig rolled in another direction, knocking her down. Water gushed past with such force that she was swept along with it, everything colored greenish gray through her stinging eyes. She clawed her way to her knees, shivering with cold, then tried to pull herself up along the lee side of the forecastle.

Jock Riordan, soaked with spray, was startled to see her. "Have you seen my brother?" she shouted over the wind. "The one who wanted your hat?"

"Is he still on deck? That devil's clip! I told him to go below five minutes ago."

"You did see him?"

"I was up in the rigging and shouted down to him to

get below where it was safe. Next time I looked he was gone."

"But he's not below!"

They stared at each other, cold faces streaked with water. The mate's big hand clamped down on the young sailor's shoulder. "Riordan, Martingale's in a bloody row with the cook. You'd better help break it up before they kill each other."

"A little boy's been lost, sir."

"He'll turn up. But you'll not find him here on deck. There's nobody left but the watch." He plunged away toward the stern.

Jock Riordan steadied Cathleen by the elbows. "Now listen, I'll look for him. Little boys can squeeze into funny small places and hide away. It's not safe for you here. Go to your parents, Cathleen."

"He's gone over the side, hasn't he?" she heard herself scream above the wind. "You know he has!"

Hours later, as the wind hushed and softened, Cathleen felt the lullaby motion of the brig as it rocked her through the longest night of her life. She couldn't sleep, or believe that she would ever sleep again. The emigrants, exhausted by sickness, snored and groaned in the moist darkness. Next to her in bed she felt her mother's breath shape silent hopeless prayers. Her father was quiet, but she knew that he was awake. Every few minutes he would turn, and a deep sigh would break out of him, more terrible than a cry.

It was all her fault. She would be punished in some awful way for what had happened to Bartley. She hoped it would be soon, something to burn away the anguish of the night. She thought again of Bartley, the comical face, the rough, deep voice, his wild spray of hair. His curiosity and questions, his scrambled attempts to decipher the universe. And the things he swallowed! Coins, hairpins, nuts and bolts—why, if you set a magnet near the boy he'd be clamped to it in a second with all the metal stuck in his belly. The things he did to himself! Smashed fingernails that turned a gruesome purple and dropped off. A big toe almost severed by an axe, and stitched on crooked. Bruises, bumps, scars, a bee sting that swelled his hand into a gassy ball. The time he sniffed a pussy willow up his nose, and all the black pepper it took, heated on the fire, to make him sneeze it out again.

Cathleen knew she was a puzzlement to her mother, and a disappointment and an irritant to her father, but she and Bartley had been friends. In a hostile world they could always make each other laugh. She could not imagine a day without Bartley; a lifetime would be unendurable. The sailor, Jock Riordan, had cared, had been kind. She was sick and cold, terribly cold, she would never be warm again. Finally she slept, because it was too painful to stay awake.

"It's for you."

The scratchy voice. Something glowing like a tiny sun swung back and forth in front of her eyes.

"It's an orange, Cathleen. The lady gave it to me for you."

"Bartley!"

"It's the lad—he's back!" Nightcapped heads popped out of upper and lower berths.

Johnny Hoult swung down from above and landed on the O'Faoláins with a thump. "Bartley's back!"

"Oh, where have you been? We thought you were drowned!" Moira O'Faoláin, her face streaked with tears, hugged and kissed and rocked Bartley back and forth. "The night we've been through, you naughty boy."

His father said, "You'll have your backside warmed proper, just wait and see."

Bartley was busy wiping off kisses, fending off jabs and pokes from Johnny Hoult, and still trying to give Cathleen the orange. "I stayed with a lady who told me about the Egyptians," he said. "They built pointy things in the sand and stuck dead people in them, with things all packed for a trip." He put the orange under his sister's nose. "Smell it—smells nice, doesn't it? I told her about the sea serpent, but she doesn't believe in it. The captain has a yellow bird, but it never sings. The lady wants to meet you, Cathleen."

9

Such a day! A brilliant sky running with clouds, and the sea green, bounding and leaping. Sleek sails fattened with wind. Sunlight and tonic air. They were still in the channel, just off the Mull of Cantire.

The emigrants, allowed the freedom of the foredeck, walked with faces reddened by the sun, making bets on how long the voyage would last.

"Twenty-five days!"

"You're an optimist, man. I've heard of ships that took seventy to make the crossing."

"And I've heard of some who have done it in twenty."

"You believe that nonsense? Sixty-two, that's my wager."

"And I say fifty, God willing."

"Thirty-five, if the weather stays fair."

Mr. Roohan, writing down the bets in a little note-book, slapped a friendly hand down on Tim Healy's shoulder. "And what'll you bet, lad?"

In spite of the racing ship and the fine, frivolous day, the boy still wore his mourning face, his sad, drowned clothing. "Sir?"

"How long do you think it will be before we catch sight of land? If you're right you'll win a gallon of rum, and a shipload of friends in the bargain."

58

"I never drink that vile stuff. It's bad for the liver and aggravates the gout."

"Not at your age, my boy. It may tickle the lover in you, but nothing worse. Come on now, you seem to be an intelligent fellow, what do you say?"

"I say our chances of reaching Canada at all aren't that bright. We're bound to run into worse storms than what we've already been through, and there's always the risk that pirates will attack and slaughter the lot of us. And if the ship fever or the cholera catches up with us, then we're done for sure. So maybe we could do it in forty-two if the captain were a saint and his crew were holy angels, but they aren't, so I doubt it."

"Forty-two it is, then." Mr. Roohan wrote it down and wandered away, looking confused and depressed.

Some of the women had spread out mildewed clothing to air in the sunshine, and every so often a shirt or a petticoat would cartwheel away in the breeze. The children had picked up the sailors' rolling strut, and no matter which way the brig tossed they managed to keep their balance. Everyone felt better, and they were able to cook food again and picnic on the foredeck. There was talk of setting up for a dance, and the surgeon, with his strange, unfocused eyes, agreed to play the fiddle for it. Just the thought of it made Cathleen feel light with excitement. She loved music; like all the good things, there had been too little of it in her life. She hoped that her father would at least let her watch, even if he were set against her joining in.

Mrs. O'Faoláin had come up from below to sit with the other women. She knitted at a stocking, keeping an eye on Bartley while the ladies chatted.

"There she is!" Bartley pointed back toward the quarterdeck, where the ship's great wheel was manned. "There's my lady."

His adventure two days before had kept him talkative for hours. He'd seen Miss Elizabeth Arnold on the day they left Dublin, when her speckled servant girl had eaten an orange, sucking it juicily and spitting the pits over the side. Later he'd made the journey to the cabin by himself, along the rain-slicked deck, over ropes, around barrels, and down the cramped companionway stairs into forbidden territory. Captain Greeley's cabin was full of rolled-up charts and maps, with an old gun hung on two brass hooks and a yellow bird swinging from the skylight. Yes, and the ivory skull of some frightening creature, which gleamed at him from the top of a carved little desk. Farther along, through another open doorway, he had seen the friendly English girl, sitting on a red velvet sofa reading a book. She'd been very surprised to see him, but had invited him in and stuffed him full of gingerbread. ("No, I didn't *ask* for any, she wanted me to have it," he'd said.) Then she had told him stories about the Egyptians and shown him a book with pictures of their long necks and enameled eyes. As the storm grew worse Minerva Flynn, her servant, had been sent to find a sailor who would take him back into steerage, but everyone was too busy, so Miss Arnold had had him on her hands all night. He'd had a lovely time, slept like a kitten on the sofa, covered with a shawl.

"Let's go talk to her, Cathleen."

"We can't. Only cabin passengers are allowed to walk on the quarterdeck."

"Why?"

"Because she paid a lot of money for her passage, and that gives her special privileges."

"She won't mind."

"She might not, but the captain most certainly will. He's already said so."

"It's not fair."

Bartley didn't know it yet, Cathleen thought, but life was an unfair contest all the way around. Poor people scraping along as best they could, dodging and ducking the blows that were bound to hit sometime. Rich people padded against misfortune. *Injustice.* That puzzled her more than anything else. Why were some born to be masters and mistresses, to wealth and luxury, while others were born to serve, to poverty and drudgery? Liddy Dillon, going out to Canada and glad of the opportunity to do the washing up for someone too lazy to do it herself. Cathleen knew that she could never be a servant to anyone. Yet simply being a woman meant a kind of servitude, didn't it? *Injustice,* all over again. Men had some choices. They could work the land, join the army, or, like Jock Riordan, go to sea. They could remain respectable bachelors, if that's what they wanted. But women grew up under a father's rule, and were handed over to another master when they married. Marriage and motherhood were the ultimate destiny. A spinster was only an economic burden on somebody else. Cathleen wished that she could be a great scholar like Doctor Johnson, read great and witty books, perhaps write one herself. But there was no chance of that, no chance for her at all. Some said that the new land was a place of great freedom and bold opportunities, but she doubted it. Hadn't she read of boatloads of black captives robbed out of Africa and sold into slavery? So even in North America the same injustices went on. And when she asked questions about these things her father only said that religion gave the proper answers.

She saw him now, standing silent and disapproving as Mr. Roohan made his joking rounds to collect the bets.

"Father? Why shouldn't I walk on the quarterdeck like the English girl?"

He glanced to where she pointed, at the tall figure of Elizabeth Arnold, whose skirts lifted lightly in the wind. "Because it's not your place, Cathleen."

"Then where is my place?"

"Why, in steerage, with us. That's where God has put you."

"Then He's made a mistake."

"Cathleen!"

"I don't belong in steerage at all. Nobody does, it's a terrible place. It's as if we're being punished for being Irish and poor, while she's being rewarded for being English and rich. So if there *is* a God, then He's mistaken."

He stared, then spoke in a rough voice thickened with anger. "Go below. Stay there until I decide what's to be done about that blistering, blasphemous tongue of yours."

"Father, it's a beautiful day. You can't send me below, for the rest of my life, every time I anger you. Please don't make me stay down there. I know I'll get sick again."

"You'll stay there until you tell me it's *you* who have made a mistake."

"I only spoke my thoughts. Why should I be punished for that?"

"You dare to question the will of God? You dare to question His existence?"

"Yes, I do. So have others!"

"I've never struck you before, Cathleen, your mother won't have it. But I'll do it here and now if you don't quickly go below."

Around them voices had grown quiet, died away. Many of the Irish stared with curiosity; some, embarrassed, looked away. Jock Riordan, splicing a rope nearby, whistled softly through his teeth. His eyes met Cathleen's as she walked quickly toward the open hatchway; they were a vivid blue, and bright with sympathy. Her cheeks went hot.

Between decks there was a packed, acrid smell of sickness and sweat that no fresh air or sunshine could ever drive out. Most of the berths were empty, but arthritic old Mrs. Gogarty lay curled, staring into empty space, her bumpy, swollen fingers plucking at her rosary.

Cathleen sat on their mattress. Far back in the depths of the steerage she heard scuffling sounds, angry voices, a sharp slap. Someone grunted and swore. Quick footsteps knocked along the wooden planks. It was Liddy Dillon, flushed in the face, her clothes all twisted and awry as if she'd slept in them. She saw Cathleen, stopped, straightened her skirts. "I thought everyone was on deck. What's the matter?"

"I'm to stay down here. My father's angry with me."

"Stay in this stinking hole? With the sun shining above? Why, that's criminal." She plopped into the berth beside Cathleen. "I'll keep you company for a few minutes, if you like. Listen, hear that? My stomach sounds as if there's thunder in it."

"Are you hungry?"

"Of course I'm hungry, aren't you? It's my natural condition. I had to use most of the money I'd saved for my passage, so there wasn't much left for provisions. I'm trying to manage on one meal a day."

"Maybe we can give you something, Liddy. But I'll have to ask my father—everything's locked up."

"No, don't you do it. You've as little as the rest of us, I'm sure. I can look out for myself, don't worry your head about that."

"I've news for you. I've heard talk. There's to be a dance later on."

"A dance? Och, isn't that grand? But there's someone who won't be dancing for a while." She laughed, and looked back in the direction from which she'd just come. A man stood squinting at them, his hands on his hips.

"Tried to tumble me, he did," Liddy whispered. "But I can take care of myself. And anyone who gets in my way."

10

For two days Cathleen had to stay between decks, out of the sunlight and the air, with only a little salt beef and biscuit to relieve the boredom. She walked back and forth the length of steerage for what seemed at least a hundred miles. Sometimes she talked to Mrs. Gogarty. The old woman lay in her berth, sighing and groaning and mumbling at her prayers. Every so often she took out the new mirror, which she had hidden under the mattress, but the face in it was so fierce and resentful that she couldn't stand the sight of it.

Her father had told her to occupy her time with the Holy Scriptures, but she refused. "Since religion got me into this mess, I can hardly expect it to get me out of it again," she said to her mother. Instead she tried to knit a worsted stocking and made a mess of it. If there was a passenger on board with a long, thin, crooked leg and a short, fat, crooked foot, then she would make him a present of it.

Bartley popped up and down the ladder, as informative as a newspaper. They were on the Atlantic now, it was dark blue, they had sighted another ship. The nice sailor, Jock Riordan, had asked after Cathleen and taught Bartley how to tie special knots. Bartley had practiced with his own laces and been so successful that they had to be cut to save him from sleeping in his boots.

Liddy visited from time to time, out of breath from the dances that thumped daily overhead. There was too little room, she said, for polkas or quadrilles, but she was content with the squeezed jigs and reels. The ship's surgeon was a strange one, addicted to laudanum, but he played the fiddle with a golden touch, like someone in a mad, drugged dream.

"The trouble with dancing," said Liddy, "is that it makes me ever so happy, but starving hungry as well. I can't give it up, but I'm likely to dance myself thin as a shillelagh before this voyage is over."

Mrs. O'Faoláin, heavy and weary in her pregnancy, sometimes stayed below to rest, but as she felt much better on the upper deck she was away with Bartley for long stretches of the day. She worried about Cathleen. "It's not good for you to be stuck away down here. It's not a wholesome place."

"Then why don't you speak for me and tell *him* so. Tell him I've done nothing wrong."

"How can I judge that, Cathleen? You've upset him—and you do have a knack for it. He says you've told him wicked things."

"Wicked things? That's foolish. What right does he have to keep me suffocating here? Why should he punish me? How can he be so certain that he's right?"

"Tell him you're sorry."

"I'm *not* sorry. And I'll not fashion a silly lie as a key out of this prison. You're my mother. Why won't you tell him to let me go?"

"He's my husband. I can't stand against him."

"Why can't you? Does marriage make a woman witless, weak, unable to reason? Well, I'll tell you something. I respect your mind and judgment more than his. I respect my own more than his. If I were his son, I'd fight him for my right to stand on deck. I would, I'd fight him!"

"Cathleen, please don't say such fierce and dreadful things."

"Mother, you're a gentle woman, and I love you for that. But you never will defend me, ever. And it's hard to stand alone all the time, it's so hard. But I can't be what I'm not." She turned away. "My head just aches and aches. Sometimes I think the world's gone truly mad, there seems so little reason in it."

When her mother went up to boil the tea water, Cathleen lay down, hoping to sleep, to blank out some of the long, lonely hours. She felt a harsh despair. She knew that her father didn't intend to be cruel. Perhaps he even felt as bad as she did. But they were two different minds and temperaments. Like scissor blades, they would always clash. She must be the first to make an apology, before he would bend at all, and this was what was so dishonest and unfair. But how long could she hold out, smothering below?

"Cathleen?" Her name urgently whispered. A touch on her shoulder. She sat upright.

"Jock! Oh, but I'm glad to see you."

"I've been worried. The way Bartley went on I expected to find you bound and gagged."

"Nothing like that. It's just a family matter."

"I can only stay for a minute. The captain doesn't like us to mix with the passengers. I'm in for it if I get caught down here."

"What's he afraid of? That you'll all be contaminated?"

"I can't speak for him, but I've no such worry since I'm Irish myself. Nothing's going to rub off on me."

They whispered together for a few minutes, expecting at any moment to be interrupted. He was eighteen, he told her, the youngest of five sons, with both parents dead. After three years at sea he still liked the life it offered. Any ship was a floating university; he could sail where he pleased, and what great, rough, exciting times he'd had. He also had an ambition. "Boys my age have been masters of ships, Cathleen. Perhaps I'll be a captain too one day." He stood close to her, smiling down. "I'd better go now. I just needed the sight of you. And here you are, so let me look."

"Why?"

"It makes me feel good, that's why. You've excitable eyes, full of sparks."

"Sparks! You're a bit mad, aren't you? What's that tattoo on your lower arm?"

Quickly he put it out of sight behind his back. "Now that you'll have to find out for yourself."

"And how will I manage it? Wrestle you down?"

He was serious now. "I wish your father hadn't left you down here by yourself. Will you be alright?"

"I will. Nothing happens here. I only wish something would."

He said, "Take care," touched her hand, and left.

She prickled pleasantly, thinking for a long while of the sailor who was concerned about her. Warm hands, disturbing eyes. Something had happened between them, something she knew her father would distrust. These feelings were new to her, and confusing, but whatever they were she knew they weren't wrong. Overhead the music started up again. Her feet beat time to it, and then she was dancing, trying to keep her balance in the cluttered center aisle.

"What are you doing down here all alone?"

She whirled. A man, thumbs hooked in his pants, stood staring at her. She recognized him. She had seen him the day Liddy Dillon had come out of the back of steerage, all rumpled and red in the face, and said he had tried to tumble her.

"I've a headache, that's all. And I'm not alone. Mrs. Gogarty's here with me."

He was dirty and nervous, with big-knuckled hands falling out of coarse shirt sleeves. When he didn't move along, Cathleen felt a twinge of fear.

"But Mrs. Gogarty don't move or talk at all," he said. "She's going to die soon."

"Shhhh, you mustn't say that. She might hear you."

He sat down on the berth and smiled at her. His face was stupid, empty, with shallow, small eyes. He grabbed her by the waist and pulled her toward him. "Well, I know a sure cure for the headache. Give us a kiss and it's gone."

"Keep your hands to yourself." She tried to push him away. "I said, *let go!*"

"Now what's the matter? Don't you like me?"

"No, I don't."

He pulled her down, sent her sprawling on the quilt. Then he fell on top of her. He was trying to kiss her, and yet he acted as if he hated her, as if he intended to do

69

something violent and terrible. She couldn't breathe or scream or move. His whiskers scraped against her cheek; she was pinned under him, his hard lips moving all over her face and neck. She twisted her head from side to side, smelling the drink on his breath, using elbows and fingernails as weapons. Ragged sounds ripped out of her throat.

"Get off her! Leave that child alone!" Over her wild, careening heart Cathleen heard Liddy's voice. "I'm going to scream so loud that every man on this boat will be down here in seconds to bash in your stupid brains. Leave her, I said! *Get off!*"

He stood up, breathing harshly, his mouth dropping open. "She asked for it," he said. "Throwing herself about. She gave me a look, I know what she was after."

"Now you listen to me," said Liddy Dillon. "If anyone finds out what you've been up to, you'll never see the other side of the Atlantic. This is a child you're fooling with, an *innocent*. And her father would kill you if he knew. Make no mistake about it, you're in terrible trouble. If there's one thing we don't need on this boat it's a bloody beating or a murder. So keep your dirty hands to yourself or we'll talk and you'll wish you'd never set eyes on either of us. Go on, get out of here."

"You can shut your stupid face," he said. "She asked for it." He walked quickly away, and disappeared up the ladder.

"I didn't ask for anything. I hate him!"

"I know . . . I know . . ." Liddy said. "Don't be all upset now, and stop your shivering. Shhhhhh . . . shhhhh." She put a strong arm around Cathleen. "It was a bad experience, for sure, but don't think on it too long or take a twisted look at other men because of it. Come on, Cathleen, don't cry so. It's over." She whispered, "There can be loving in a man's touch, you'll discover that for yourself one day, and this will just be a tattered old nightmare. This was . . . oh, my dear . . . it was just unfortunate."

"But I feel so ashamed. And what shall I tell my father?"

Liddy bristled, "Tell him what happened. Perhaps it will shake some sense into his thick head. Keeping you penned down here, like a common thief or worse! But don't identify the man unless you feel you must. I know what will happen to him, and I've seen enough brutality and bloodshed in my time to last me forever. He'll not bother you again, I promise."

"I really think my father would do something terrible to him."

"You see? But it proves, in a way, that he does care for you after all. Come up with me now, Cathleen. You're not staying down here another blessed minute."

11

Nine days out of Dublin. It seemed longer than that, they had passed through such a variety of weather. There had been no more of the rough squalls that had flattened them with seasickness at the outset, but the days, like a pack of Gypsy cards, had been dealt in a shuffling succession of good and bad—windy sunshine, unexpected hail and snow, some rain and fog. Now, late in May, a strong breeze drove out of the east and sent the *Fair Western Lady* skidding madly across the water. The emigrants were cheered with fresh hopes of a short passage and an early arrival in Quebec.

It was the Sabbath. Early that morning a small group had assembled on deck to observe it. Washed and neatly dressed, they had started prayers when Captain Greeley ordered them below to carry up their bedding.

"Why must it be aired today?" It was Liam O'Faoláin who spoke for the others.

"As a health measure." The captain flapped the Rules and Regulations Act that he carried with him at all times.

"It seems to me that you only enforce what suits you and ignore the rest. We've asked you for several days now to allow us to air out the bedding, the steerage smells so foul. But only on the Sabbath do you agree to it." Mr. O'Faoláin confronted the captain, face to face. "Can it not be done on any other day as well? Can't we have prayers in the open air this morning?"

"Sunday suits my schedule. I always have it done then. It's customary when the weather's fit."

Cathleen saw that most of the emigrants were awed by the captain. Greeley was a difficult man, with a tough job and a rough crew. It was his nature to give orders and to make sure those orders were obeyed. He didn't attempt to be kind to his crew nor to anyone else. What little kindness was in him he squeezed out upon Harvey, the yellow bird that dangled from the cage in his cabin. A rumor, spread by Thomas, the ship's steward, was that the captain petted the bird with his finger, pursed up his lips, and made kissing sounds into the cage, but nobody else had seen such a thing, or believed it was possible. The captain's reputation was a hard one, and this pleased him very much. To enhance the image, he wore a set of brass knuckles bent into the shape of monkeys, and these fit the bottom of his hand like a smooth and nasty glove. Rubbing, rubbing, he polished them constantly on sleeves, jacket, trouser legs, a gleaming threat always in sight. Another symbol of his power was the old blunder-buss displayed on the wall of his cabin. Once he had killed an albatross with it, and the skull stared out from the top of his desk, an amazed ivory ornament.

As the emigrants carried up bundles of quilts and coverlets, one of the blankets was torn away in the grip of the wind. It belonged to a palsied old lady from county Clare and was a sad loss to her, but as it soared away like a sail the first mate laughed.

"Hoo there—Miss Arnold! It's me, Bartley!"

Cathleen looked up, saw the young girl on the afterdeck wave a hand in their direction.

"May I go see her, Cathleen?"

"No, stay here, Bartley, and help me." Cathleen spread the bedding in the sunshine, relaxing in the freedom of the upper deck. They had grown used to the endless creaking of the brig, the monotonous pattern of cooking, eating, sleeping, and caring for the children. There was singing and courting and quarrels. Letters from relatives and friends who had already settled were exchanged, along with bits and pieces of information. Nearby, Mr. Hoult, who couldn't read, grinned while his son read for him. The boy stumbled over the words, his finger fumbling underneath the written lines. " 'We are in the land of liberty, with no . . . tithes . . . taxes . . . no rates. Farmers have no rent to pay . . . because they farm their own land.' "

As the boy read, Cathleen was aware of Jock Riordan, who seemed to be fore and aft at the same time, joking with the crew, fooling with the children, noisy in the rigging. Whenever the captain was below, Jock managed to collect an audience. He was a magician, a sleight-of-hand artist. Coins poured out every time he squeezed Bartley's nose. Seeing Cathleen on deck again, he went into a pantomime of exaggerated joy and relief, and she laughed out loud at the sight of him.

Mr. Gogarty's thin voice trembled as he read news from a married daughter, settled in Upper Canada. " 'The longer we live here, the better things become!' Did you hear that? She says, 'We've got a hundred acres of land, four clear already.' "

One end of a quilt, tied to the stays, came loose.

Cathleen caught it in time, waltzed with it briefly in the wind, pinned it back in place.

"We shall have tea and meat for breakfast, and for dinner and for supper too," Mrs. Hoult wheezed. "It's the custom there, I've heard. Just imagine that!"

Conversation stopped as the first mate, respectfully called Mr. Mate by the Irish, took an observation through the eyehole of the quadrant. The emigrants thought he must be a humorous man, because he laughed so much. Cathleen saw that he only laughed when something unfortunate happened. A ducking, smashed crockery, a loss of rations, a scalding—any of these was sure to set him roaring.

Mr. Roohan had climbed to the top of the forecastle, and he balanced there, enjoying the broader panorama of the sea. Jock crept quietly up on him and drew a circle in chalk around the old man's feet. The emigrants grinned, nudging each other. Some of them knew this was an old sea custom, that the victim couldn't step down until he'd "paid his footing." Mr. Roohan heard the laughter, discovered the joke, and, pretending to be angry, chased Jock the length and breadth of the vessel before he ran out of breath. Then he bought grog for the crew and said, yes, indeed, he'd gladly join them in a friendly glass, he hadn't had a moment's sickness since he'd started drinking it.

Cathleen saw how much the sailors enjoyed the break in the routine. Two mates, thirteen seamen, and three boy apprentices, the crew was occupied day and night, constantly adjusting and mending sail, polishing brass, splicing rope, spinning yarn, swabbing the deck. She knew that some of them, scraped up from dockside at the last moment and tossed like refuse into the bucket of the ship, were criminals, with robberies, assaults, maybe murders in their past. But not all of them were vicious. Some were loners and drifters, some simply loved to ride the sea, and others, like Jock, were only young, with an itch for adventure tingling under their skins. Doctor Jones, the black cook, had once been a slave, and it had broken him. Now the galley gave him a sweet power, his indigestible stews a sour revenge.

Mr. O'Faoláin stopped to speak to Cathleen. "Mind you keep your eyes on that bedding. We can't afford to lose any."

"I will."

He looked troubled. "I've been bothered ever since you told me about the man who molested you. I want you to tell me who he is. He must be dealt with."

"He's been warned already, Father. It won't happen again."

"I shouldn't have been so foolish as to leave you alone below, and I'm sorry for that. It never occurred to me such a thing might happen. But the punishment was for your own good, you realize that, don't you?"

In other days she might have said nothing, in order not to provoke him even more. Now she said, "No, I don't see how it was for my own good. But let's leave that be."

He stared at her, tense, puzzled, annoyed. "You're a forward, strange girl. There's a wildness in you sometimes, I swear I don't understand it." Still worried, "Perhaps you encouraged this man, Cathleen, without knowing it."

His suspicious nature, his distrust of her, the slash of judgment in those black brows, how sick it made her feel.

"I didn't encourage him. That's a terrible thing to say to me. I hated the very sight of him. You think you know me, but you don't, you never will. And I won't ever discuss this again. Not ever."

12

"Have you seen it?" Tim asked Cathleen.

"The shark? We've all seen it."

"It's a sign of death, you know. Sharks always follow a ship when they smell disease."

"They'd follow an elephant if they saw one. It's just to break the monotony, that's why they do it."

Yet she had felt uneasy when the shark was sighted slicing after the brig, early in the morning. A child had wailed all night, keeping her awake, and just at dawn two of the Russell children had turned feverish and started to cry. The surgeon came down and examined them and said it was the measles. Fifteen or twenty of the emigrants were suffering from dysentery, and for them he advised flour porridge with laudanum to help the cramps. Nobody had any laudanum; the only medical supplies the emigrants had brought were rhubarb pills, Epsom salts, and castor oil. And nobody had much faith in his remedies anyway, since they'd learned he wasn't a surgeon after all, but an apothecary's assistant who only wanted a free passage across the Atlantic.

It was warm and muggy below, and the stench was fierce. Cathleen was glad to go on deck to fix the stirabout, made from the siftings of oatmeal. Mrs. O'Faoláin, gray in the face and breathless, brought

Bartley along for the fresh air. He'd broken out with boils on his buttocks and complained loudly that he couldn't sit down.

"I'll fix a poultice," she said. "But I don't know what the fuss is about, since you never sit down for two minutes a day as it is."

A fine mist drifted across them as they waited their turn at the fire grate. The day's rations were given out to the emigrants who had contracted for them, and there were the usual bitter complaints about the meager portions. Then Mrs. Roohan, who had brought up an egg to fry for her husband, was jostled by a spiteful woman who would have liked it for her own, and the egg splattered on the deck. The two women tore around and around the longboat, the chickens squawking in terror, while Mrs. Roohan called on the holy saints to help her catch and punish the offender.

Another argument broke out when the water was distributed at eleven o'clock. As Mr. O'Faoláin collected his family's supply he abruptly lost his temper. The water had been taken from the filthy Dublin harbor some time before the brig set sail, and it had never been pleasant. But after less than two weeks it had turned muddy and bitter from being stored in old wine casks. Mr. O'Faoláin, as Head of the Committee, asked to speak to the captain, and when they were face to face, he held the can out to be examined.

"What is it now, O'Faoláin, another complaint?"

"This water, Captain. The stuff's undrinkable."

"What's the matter with it?"

"It was bad at the start, for one thing, and there's no

excuse for that. And now it looks as if all of Ireland's poor had been rinsed in it, and it smells twice as bad as the lot of them. We won't have it."

Calmly, Captain Greeley took the container and turned it upside down, pouring the contents on the deck. "Then unless you've a fancy for seawater, which I believe some madmen do, you can go without today. And think it over again before tomorrow." The grating voice carried clearly to the foredeck, where the emigrants listened. "Now, I have heard your complaints about my cook, and the price of my grog, and the behavior of my men toward your *delicate* and *refined* women, and my interruption of your prayers, and I tell you, O'Faoláin, I'm sick of them."

"It's my function to see that our rights are enforced."

"Not on my brig. You and your scum! There's no law says I have to pet and coddle you filthy Irish across the Atlantic Ocean. You fuss over trifles while there isn't one among you knows how to keep decent and clean. You're already crawling with vermin, your men are drunks, your women are whores."

"You're a liar!"

"Go to the devil, O'Faoláin. I'll hear no more about it. Drink the water or not, it's all the same to me." As he stamped away, the second mate, a mild little man with childish, sad eyes who never spoke above a whisper, said, "We all drinks it, we're used to it. But there's ways to fix it, you know. Boil it up with a pinch of tea, or put charcoal in it. Alum will do, if you have it. Or vinegar."

"Maybe it's the vinegar that's turned your captain so sour," Cathleen said, smiling at him. She sat with her mother on deck, knitting. She hated knitting, it was such torture. She wondered what demented soul had thought it up in the first place. Worsted flowed through Mrs. O'Faoláin's fingers as she kept one eye on her own work and another on Bartley, who wrestled nearby with some of the other boys. A young woman, newly married, said, "That son of yours, Mrs. O'Faoláin, is a torment to me, you may as well know it."

"What's he done then, Mrs. Rourke?"

"It's nothing he's done to me, mind. It's just his continual agitation from dawn until dark, tongue wagging the whole time and never stopping. He'll have it worn out before he's half grown. It's a parcel of triplets you have there, rolled up into one boy, and it makes me very nervous. I'm a sensitive person, everyone remarks how sensitive I am, and that boy drives me to distraction."

"He's naturally high-spirited and full of energy." There was a hard edge to Moira O'Faoláin's usually serene voice. "Considering the space we have, he runs it off harmlessly enough, I think."

"You might use some control over him, for the peace of mind of others."

"Mrs. Rourke." The flashing needles stopped, suspended in the air. "If you have a specific complaint, I'm quite willing to hear it. But if you're annoyed because Bartley is Bartley, then there's nothing I can do about that."

The Portuguese seaman sat nearby, legs stretched out before him, using the leather sailor's palm to push a needle through heavy canvas as he mended sail. In a mysterious, haunted accent he told stories of phantom ships, disastrous fires at sea, and killer sharks while Tim

Healy listened raptly. Cathleen's attention wandered from her mangled knitting. Jock Riordan was tightening backstays, and she saw again the tattoo on his lower arm. She wondered if it might be the name of a sweetheart. Oh, the silly things people did in the name of love! What would possess a man to carve up his arm with a woman's name, when five minutes later he might want to forget her? Cathleen laughed at herself for being indignant at Jock when his tattoo might be a two-headed baboon for all she knew. He saw her then and, with a flash of a smile, dropped his marlinespike. It was a sharp instrument used for splicing rope, and it just missed parting the first mate's hair as he walked below. The air quivered with curses as he ordered Jock to come down and be strangled. Jock immediately climbed higher into the rigging, flung a hand across his eyes, and swore he sighted land. Everybody laughed, and the first mate, bloated with anger, was fortunately called below.

Bartley ran up. "Miss Arnold wants to talk to you, Cathleen."

"Don't be fooling me."

"I'm not. She does. She sent me to fetch you."

"Then tell your lady that since I can't walk on the quarterdeck or go to her cabin, she'll have to come to me."

Bartley memorized breathily, ". . . can't walk on the quarterdeck . . . or cabin . . . better come on here," and ran off again.

"He has a fascination for that English girl," said their mother. "Whether it's her oranges or her Egyptians, I'm not entirely sure. And none of the ship's rules seem to apply to him. He just runs where he pleases."

"Perhaps if the ship's log were applied to his other end," Mrs. Rourke was quick to put in, "then he'd not run so free."

The two women turned away from each other, knitting fiercely. In a few minutes Bartley was back, followed by the cabin passenger.

"Miss O'Faoláin? I'm Elizabeth Arnold."

"Yes, Bartley has told me about you."

"May we talk privately?"

Cathleen looked about at the cramped deck packed with emigrants. "We can try," she said. The Irish women stared, with quick, envious glances, at Elizabeth Arnold's well-fitted dress, the pearl ring on her finger, her elegant leather boots. As they moved toward the bulwarks, Cathleen saw that the English girl wasn't much older than herself. She had a settled maturity about her, as if she'd been pickled in infancy into something elderly and wise beyond her years. Her face was long and plain, with a thin strand of nose set in the middle. She had intelligent, large eyes, and the lovely blossoming English skin.

"I have a problem. I hope you can help me."

"What is it, Miss Arnold?"

"It's my girl, Minerva Flynn. She's been ill since yesterday, and the surgeon thinks it might be cholera. I'm really very concerned."

"I shouldn't wonder. Can she be helped?"

"He isn't very hopeful, and she does seem to be getting worse. But I'm sure she'll recover, I know she will." Elizabeth hesitated. "I'm so fond of Minerva. She's more of a companion to me than anything else. The truth is,

I'm not very experienced with sick people, and I'm rather frightened. I don't know what to do."

"I'll go along with you, then, and see if there's any way I can help."

Cathleen stopped to tell her mother where she was going, and to warn Bartley that Minerva Flynn was sick and that he mustn't go to the passenger cabin. Then she followed the tall young woman down the companionway stairs.

13

The lady's cabin was a cramped little area with a berth on either side, a red velvet sofa squeezed in between. The sofa, scruffy and faded, was the only suggestion of elegance on the entire brig, and it struck Cathleen as pretentious and comical. There was a small deal table piled with books, books stacked on each end of the sofa, and more on a shelf that was recessed into the wall.

Minerva Flynn lay in the berth to the right, her face so white that all the freckles showed, like pepper spilled on a tablecloth. Her eyes were sunken and the skin around her lips was blue. As they came into the cabin she cried out in pain.

Elizabeth said, "It started with vomiting and hiccuping. She's exhausted now, and she has cramps in her legs and feet that hurt her terribly."

Minerva's eyes were open. Her light hair, darkened with sweat, streaked the pillow. Her dry lips moved to shape a word, and she tried to raise herself.

"I'm sure she wants a drink, but when I give it to her she chokes."

"Let's try again." Cathleen put an arm around the sick girl and helped steady her. Elizabeth offered water, but after a sip Minerva retched and dropped back on the pillow. Her expression was anxious, pitiful. She drew up her legs beneath the bedding and cried out in a husky voice, "What did I do with it? I've lost it, and I won't ever find it."

Elizabeth took her hand. "What have you lost? I'll help you look for it."

Minerva lay quietly. A faint knock came at the door, and the surgeon drifted in. He examined the girl, and then, as if he spoke from a distant empty room, he said, "There's nothing more to be done."

"But you've done nothing at all! Surely there's something that will make her more comfortable, that might help her get well again." Elizabeth drew him aside, whispered, "She *will* recover, won't she?"

"It's a matter of time. You'll soon know one way or the other."

"What good is he? Oh, what good is he!" she said, when he had gone. During the afternoon she paced, back and forth, stopping every few minutes to stare down into Minerva's face, and to ask Cathleen, "Do you think she's improving?" Minerva's skin was lax and clammy. She spoke only after long silent intervals, murmuring about a brooch she had misplaced and was certain she would never find again.

Cathleen sat beside her, remembering how her own mother had soothed her through her childhood illnesses, and found herself repeating the same comforting words. "You're going to be just fine. Rest now, and you'll feel much better in the morning. Don't worry, we're here with you, soon you'll be right as summer rain."

The steward brought in a tray of food. Thomas was thirteen and lazy, with a sweet, amiable smile and a nervous twitch from ducking the first mate, who cuffed him whenever he saw him. "I beg your pardon, Miss Arnold, but since she's sick and won't feel like eating anything, could I have what's left?" He nudged the tray onto the table, keeping an awed distance from Minerva.

"If there's anything left, Thomas, of course you may have it."

"Thank you, Miss Arnold." He rubbed his head, ducked, and shone his smile on them. "Sometimes I think I wouldn't mind being sick and lying in bed with people saying nice, soft things to me."

When he had shuffled out, with a last anxious glance at Minerva, Elizabeth sighed. "Poor Thomas. Everyone abuses him and beats him, he's so useless. And food is his only comfort. It's all he ever thinks about. Sometimes he tells me his dreams, all about hams and puddings, such sweet and greasy dreams." She gestured toward the tray. "Cathleen, if you're hungry, please take something."

For days Cathleen had eaten small portions of stir-about, an occasional piece of salt beef, and the incredibly hard ship's biscuit. The smell of boiled mutton was irresistible. "But I feel so guilty. For eating not just Minerva's dinner, but Thomas's as well."

"Don't worry about it. I take good care of Thomas."

Elizabeth ate very little herself. She had a large store of Madeira in the cabin, and she opened a bottle and poured the wine into two tiny crystal glasses that she kept in a padded box in her trunk. "I'd heard how dreadful the water is at sea, so I'm prepared to drink as little of it as possible."

A lantern sent drunken shadows reeling around the

cabin walls, and Cathleen realized that it was evening.

"You will stay with me tonight?" Elizabeth asked. "I don't want to be alone."

"Yes, of course I'll stay." She saw that the English girl was very frightened, and unable to cope with the situation.

It was very strange to be in the small private cabin sipping Madeira while a young girl who might be losing life searched for something lost within her mind. Strange, frightening, unreal. For a long time there was only silence. Cathleen thought it might help if they talked, and she questioned Elizabeth, who began to pace again, working out her anxiety in a nervous flow of words.

"Four years ago," she said, "my father decided to go out to Canada. I don't know why . . . I think he fancied himself the country gentleman and decided he could play the role less expensively there than in England. So now he indulges himself in the things he most enjoys—drinking, hunting, and fishing. In that order." She bent over Minerva, touched her hand, said to Cathleen, "See how quiet she is. Do you think she looks a little better?" Again she walked back and forth. "He's rather old, my father. Very severe and unapproachable." She straightened, made herself look like a haughty portrait, and then smiled. "Like that. I've always been afraid of him. But then, I think he's always been a little afraid of me. When I was small he saw that I liked to read and study, so he provided me with excellent tutors. Tutors took up my time, and books kept me quiet and out of his way. He kept me well supplied with books." Cathleen saw that she wasn't bitter, only direct and factual. "Then when he went off to Canada he sent me to an old aunt in Dublin.

That was an experience! I believe she was mad. She never went out of the house, because she was afraid of feathers, and, after all, the world is full of birds. I think she made me a little mad, too." Elizabeth stopped pacing. "Well, she's dead now, God rest her eerie soul. And I do hope angels *don't* have wings, they'll drive her to distraction."

"Your father . . . Does he like Canada? Is he happy there?"

"I don't think he's managing well. The grand estate he'd hoped for is nothing more than a lot of uncleared bush. And he complains that the servants are too free and democratic, which probably means that they want more wages than he's willing to pay. He's only written me a few letters, but I gather from what he's said that nobody is much impressed with his manners or his hunting skills or even with his beautiful English boots, which are his greatest vanity. I'm sure he's bored and lonely and disappointed. And wondering what to do with me on his hands. We'll have a time of it, I expect."

"What will you do, then, in such a lonely place?"

"I'm not sure. I'd like to persuade my father to work the land and make a real farm of it. There'd be a satisfaction, wouldn't there, in breaking fresh land, growing healthy crops? But he won't, he has no ambition for that. As for me, I've always been content to have my books about. But that doesn't seem enough anymore." Her face twisted with a sudden, surprising anger. "How wasted women are! What good are my studies if they can't be applied, passed on to somebody else? I'd love to teach. I'd be a good teacher. I taught Minerva how to read and write. She used to mimic everything I did and said, she was so timid and unsure of herself. But when she learned how to read, how to use books, then she wasn't afraid to have her own opinions. She grew so fond of Donne, and absolutely hated *Pilgrim's Progress*." Elizabeth laughed at the memory, picked up Minerva's hand, and held it tightly. "I was proud of you for that, Minerva. It made me so happy when you learned to think for yourself. I didn't feel so useless."

"When you marry, Miss Arnold, you won't have time to worry about feeling useless."

"I'll never marry. I've never seen a happy marriage. Besides, the very idea terrifies me. Bearing children, for instance. I couldn't! But then, I'm terrified of most things, Cathleen." She whispered, "Of things that creep and crawl . . . of illness and death . . . of darkness . . . but only things in the real world. Nothing in books surprises or upsets me." Again she began to pace. "No, that's not really true. Something I read recently *did* upset me. *Nothing like the misery of the Irish people exists under the sun!* Is that true?"

Cathleen said that yes, she believed it was true. She spoke of the famine objectively, as if it had happened to somebody else, trying to keep the bitterness out of her voice as she described the life of the Irish tenant farmer, his dependency year by year on the potato crop. The indifference, the inept English policy when the crops did fail. She talked, with warmth, of her mother and of her sister Eileen, who had died.

"And I've a wonderful aunt, she's that clever and gay. She's married well and lives in Limerick. All my life she's sent me books and told me I must educate myself since there's not a soul who will do it for me. She says Ireland's greatest enemy isn't famine or poverty or even the English, if you'll pardon me for saying so, but ignorance." And Cathleen added, "I believe that."

They had talked themselves out. They were tired.

14

Minerva Flynn, dead at seventeen, of cholera. Early in the morning Cathleen gently covered the body, and told a staring Thomas to notify both the captain and the surgeon. When the burial arrangements had been made she wondered what else she could do for Elizabeth Arnold. The girl was pathetic in her shock and sorrow. She rocked herself back and forth on the sofa, unable to rest or eat. "Please don't leave me, Cathleen."

"But I really must get back soon, Miss Arnold. My mother is expecting a baby, you see, and I have to help take care of Bartley."

"What will I do? I can't stay here alone!"

"I'm sure, with a little time, you'll be able to manage."

"Please, would you ask your parents if you could stay on here in the cabin. It won't be difficult, and I'll pay good wages. You may visit them whenever you like." She clutched Cathleen's arm. "Promise you'll ask."

"Alright. I will."

She had been only one night away, but the sight, the sound, the smell of steerage hit with the impact of an angry fist. She plunged back into the seething restlessness, the continual weary crying of the children, hearing again the shrill voices of irritable women. Emigrants lay in their berths, some sick with fever, others merely wretched or bored. For the first week the Committee had helped keep things orderly and clean and had rounded up volunteers to help scrub and supervise. Now it was resented and ignored. Each day brought fresh quarrels, thefts, assaults. One of the chickens that the cook kept under the longboat had been strangled and eaten. As a punishment the captain stopped all dancing on deck for a week and raised the price of his grog.

Amidst the disorder of strewn garbage, soiled bedding, and scattered possessions, the O'Faoláins' berth was a tidy oasis. Moira O'Faoláin held Bartley clamped down with one hand and applied a poultice to his boils with the other.

"Ah, the poor girl dead," she said, when Cathleen told her about Minerva. "And the infection spreading here. Three others ill with fever this morning, and more cases of measles, too." She struggled to keep Bartley pinned down. "If you don't stop that wriggling, there'll be more than boils on your backside, there'll be blisters as well. Sit on his legs, Cathleen, and make him behave."

"Miss Arnold is very anxious. Captain Greeley wants to get rid of the body right away, without any religious ceremony."

"When is it to be done?"

"As soon as they bring Minerva up on deck."

"What will they do with her?" Bartley's face was muffled in the pillow.

"She'll be buried in the sea."

His imagination wrestled with the awful fact. "May I watch them drop her in?"

"You may not!" Mrs. O'Faoláin let him sit up and pull on his trousers. "I'll speak to Liam. Perhaps he could say a few words at the burial."

93

It was damp and cold above. Fog, white as parchment, rolled across the bulwarks. Awed and curious, the emigrants watched as the body of the young girl was brought up from the cabin. Jock Riordan and the Portuguese sailor carried her wrapped in a shroud made from an old piece of sail. Tim Healy, a black warning stroke, leaned at the rail. "What did I tell you," he whispered to Cathleen. "The shark was a sign, after all."

Elizabeth Arnold stood alone, shivering under the heavy folds of her shawl. When the body had been lowered to the deck, Jock said to her, "I'm sorry for your troubles."

It was Irish comfort, spoken to the bereaved at wakes. The English girl seemed startled by his sympathy, and grateful for it. As she thanked him Cathleen thought how strangely and quickly events took place at sea. Yesterday Jock had played the clown, demanding that Mr. Roohan "pay his footing." Today he had assumed a man's burden, as a pallbearer.

Silence, dense and cold as the climate. Moisture dripped from ropes and stays as Liam O'Faoláin stepped forward and murmured some prayers. It was a phantom ceremony, his face appearing and disappearing in the flow of fog.

"Few of us knew Minerva Flynn. But her mistress tells me that she was a good, kind girl, came from a large family, thirteen in all, out of Dublin. Well, Minerva here set sail, as we all did, with high hopes for a new and better life ahead. She had youth and health, a fine, strong, comely girl she was. But all unaware, she carried with her that criminal contagion, cholera. And it killed her. What a pity," he said, "what a terrible pity. But we are all fellow voyagers, and not for this passage alone, but in the precarious life we share. For some of us . . . for Minerva here . . . the voyage is short. But for all of us, fair weather or foul, the destination is the same. It is fitting that we should gather and pray for Minerva Flynn. She should not be sent on, friendless and alone, into the dark night, into the dark sea, and into her final rest. Let us pray for her. May God have mercy on her soul, may God have mercy on us all."

Cathleen looked down at the wrapped body, parceled out in coarse canvas, and trembled. With an odd clutch of emotion she realized that her father had expressed more tenderness and compassion for the young stranger than he had ever shown toward her. In the chilled silence that followed his words, pale hands made the sign of the cross. Cathleen wiped at her face, looked up, saw Jock Riordan staring at her. Then Mr. Roohan began to cough, unable to stop himself. The sailors picked up the body, and lowered it over the side of the brig. It was a particular sound none of them had heard before. In time they would grow used to it.

Later Cathleen sat on their berth, tired out from the long night she had spent in the death watch. The scene around her was sickening. Filth everywhere, clothing and cookware in a jumble. Potatoes, rotted by seawater, paved the center aisle like cobblestones. Toward the stern, where the endless card game was played, a candle was carelessly stuck against the side of the ship, a blink of yellow through the smoke. Men disobeyed regulations and lit lucifer matches to set fires to their stinking pipes. They chewed tobacco, spat out the juice anywhere, slopped up rum. Why was it all so foul and disorganized?

Was it simply because they were Irish and ignorant as Captain Greeley said? Or was it because, penned below, bullied, and treated with contempt, they had lost self-respect.

She must ask her parents if she might attend Elizabeth Arnold in the cabin. She was sure, once she did ask, that they would urge her to go. And, thinking it over, she knew that she must take up the offer, that the wages would be a godsend to the family. Life in the privacy of the passenger cabin was comfortable and clean and, compared to the steerage, a luxury. She liked Elizabeth Arnold. At first she had appeared older and wiser, more balanced than Cathleen, but later, as her fears and helplessness were exposed, she had seemed younger and more vulnerable. Still, something touched Cathleen's pride, knotted her decision to speak. She had promised herself she would never be a servant, and now to wait upon a girl her own age, and an English one at that!

Mr. O'Faoláin moved up and down the aisle, trying to prod the listless Irish out of their beds. "You're not sick, McEwen. But if you lie there all day you soon will be—or dead."

"I'll do as I please, O'Faoláin. Do you think being Head gives you divine rights?"

"I only want you to stay fit, and to help clean up this mess."

"You don't like the looks of my rubbish? Well, I don't like the looks of your great, ugly nose, always poking into other people's business."

All she needed was a little time.

15

Liddy Dillon picked her way through the clutter. At the start of the voyage there had been a special polish to her, but since then she had lost weight, her skin had become an unpleasant color, and the conversational sauce she served up had less flavor, more bite.

"Well, Cathleen, I hear you've moved up in the world. To the lady's cabin, if you please."

"And back again, for the time being at least. How are you?"

"Well enough. But my timbers, what a mess we've got ourselves into. Did you ever imagine anything as bad as this? Why, if I died and went straight to Hell it would certainly be an improvement on these accommodations. You know, some of us were told before we sailed that the crossing might only take three weeks or so, when all the time the captain knew it would be twice that or longer. And now he'll make a great profit on those who didn't provision themselves proper, for they'll have to buy from the ship's stores. Lord, I'm almost out of food already, and I've little money on hand to buy anything from him."

"Then we'll share with you, Liddy."

"No, I'd never consent to that. No sense in having you starve, too. Besides, there are ways of getting by. I just have to make up my mind to it."

"What ways?"

"Oh, well, if you're friendly to certain people, they'll look out for you. It's kind of a bargain, do you see?"

"What people? I don't understand what you mean."

Liddy said, "Men need a woman's company now and then. They get lonely. You know how it is."

Cathleen didn't know how it was at all. Intuitively she felt that Liddy was involved in something inevitable, adult, and sad. But Liddy's serious mood lifted suddenly, the green eyes flashed. "Oh, if we could only have a dance! This miserable fog. How can they tell where we're going by squinting through a little hole in a thingamajig? I think all that measuring and reckoning is just for show anyway. They might as well look through the hole in my stocking for all the good it does."

It was just after the midday meal that the *Fair Western Lady* broke through the last panels of mist into a radiant afternoon. A strong breeze plumped the topgallant and royal sails, and sunshine flowed, working its wonders. Passengers crowded the foredeck to watch stormy petrels teeter low over the waves, dolphins soar after shoals of flying fish. Far to the east a whale blew, causing great excitement.

It was young Mrs. Rourke's twenty-first birthday, and an impromptu party developed. She was presented with a charred cake, raw in the middle, the best that could be managed on the smoldering fire grate. There was singing, and kissing, and rum passed hand to hand, and Mr. O'Faoláin was sent by his wife to extricate Bartley from the middle of the celebration before it turned into a brawl. Brawl or not, Cathleen was drawn to the sound of the joking and laughter, the sight of men and women crowded together, eating and talking and touching, and she wanted to be a part of it, not just a spectator. Then she saw the lonely figure of Elizabeth Arnold walking on the quarterdeck, and she felt ashamed. It had only been a few hours since Minerva Flynn had been buried at sea.

Mrs. O'Faoláin handed her the key to the supply chest. "Will you bring up the tea things, Cathleen? I'm dragging today with the backache."

On her way back with the kettle, Jock Riordan stopped her. "Too bad about the Flynn girl."

"Yes," she said, "it's a terrible thing." She told him she had been there when the death occurred. "Miss Arnold wants me to take Minerva's place in the cabin."

"Will you go?"

"I've not asked my parents yet."

"If you do, we won't see as much of each other . . . I mean, have the chance to talk as easily."

"I know."

He whispered, "It's warm today. The hatches will be open all night. Meet me on deck at eleven o'clock."

"I can't!"

"I know you *can't*. But I think you *will*."

"And I think you really are daft."

He grinned, and moved away from her, and she thought about him for the rest of the afternoon. What kind of a larky boy was he, then, thinking she would meet with him, like a conspirator, in the middle of the night? But he was such a pleasure to look at, that was certain, with hair so black, and the wild, blue Irish eyes, and a body all shifting grace. Warm hands. But the nonsense he told Bartley, the jokes and riddles and silly tales, and Bartley swallowed them all the way a fish takes bait. Magic tricks, sleight of hand, what did that tell of him?

Passengers formed the lines for cooking the evening meal. They were good-humored, hungry from fresh air and exercise. Cathleen went down again, to get food for their supper.

The spotted faces of the Russell children watched her wanly from their upper berth.

"We saw a whale today," she called up to them. "So get over your measles as fast as you can, and maybe we'll see another before long. They blow water away up into the air from a hole in the top of their heads." This information properly stunned them.

She was reaching for the key to the supply chest, which hung on a string around her neck, when she realized that the chest was already unlocked. She flung the lid open—and saw that everything inside was scrambled and upset: tea and sugar spilled loose, the few potatoes, the chunk of fat salt pork, the biscuit, and the oatmeal gone.

"Dear God," she repeated over and over again to herself, "I'm sorry for all the wicked things I've ever done, but don't punish the rest of the family for my faults. Don't let the food be stolen, please, God." She tried to think clearly, to reconstruct what had happened. She had come down earlier to fetch the kettle and the tea things, and she had unlocked the chest. What then? Yes, she'd been trying to remember the words to a poem by Blake that Aunt Wig had sent to her in a little book. She had remembered them at last.

> Every night and every morn
> Some to misery are born.
> Every morn and every night
> Some are born to sweet delight.

Remembered the words, and forgotten to lock up the chest.

There was secret, stifled laughter. She glanced up. The Russell children ducked their heads back out of sight.

"Did you see anyone take things from our supply chest?"

"We didn't see nothing."

What else was missing? Cathleen climbed into the berth, ran her hands frantically along the line of nails where the utensils, clothing, and tools were hung in place. Everything appeared to be there. She put her hands under the straw mattress, on the side where she slept. The sixpenny mirror was gone.

16

Her father's anger was frozen and contained, an icy statement. "Such carelessness, Cathleen, can't be excused. We'll all suffer for it. You can't be trusted, ever again." His thick boots clattered up and down between the double tiers of berths as he raised his voice above the chatter of the passengers.

"I ask you . . . beg you . . . to please return the stolen food to my family." There was a gradual quieting among the emigrants. "Don't you see what will happen if we turn one against the other, prey upon each other? Why, we'll be beasts in a jungle, each out for himself— only a few will survive. If we lose heart now, because of illness or treachery or thievery, then we'll lose more than we can spare. We'll lose our lives."

From the upper berth Mortimer Russell gestured like a preacher, his mouth soundlessly mimicking Liam O'Faoláin's words, while his brothers and sisters rolled on their blankets, smothering their laughter.

"We must help each other, be a solace and a comfort, not a threat, don't you understand that?"

The mood of the day had been spoiled, soured by the serious nature of the theft. Things had been stolen before—small articles, loose change, cooking utensils— but no family had had its entire food supply taken. In silence the Irish sullenly prepared for bed.

Bartley was already asleep, his spray of hair sticking up over the edge of the blanket. Cathleen, undressing awkwardly, caught Johnny Hoult watching her again; suddenly tears filled her eyes, and she ducked under the covers. The words "You can't be trusted, ever again" rang in her head, a jangling that wouldn't stop. Everything her father thought of her was true.

Next to her in bed her mother lay on her back, her hands folded on the rising mound of her stomach. "Cathleen?"

"Yes."

"Listen, we'll manage. We've a little saved for the new land. We'll use it to buy some supplies from the captain."

Cathleen could barely talk for the ache in her throat. "I'm sorry, *sorry* for what I did."

"I know. Stop worrying. You're not a bad girl at all. Forgetful sometimes. And young. Why, when I was a wee girl I took a gold ring to play with that belonged to a proud aunt. And lost it, of course. To this very day I'll remember the way I felt, as if there was a needle stuck through my heart. But things always seem worse at night than they really are." Shyly she touched Cathleen's shoulder. "You'll feel better tomorrow."

Cathleen swallowed. Her eyes burned with tears, and she couldn't say another word. An argument rumbled behind the partition at the stern. Cathleen heard her father ask the men to put away their drink and cards and go to bed so that others could sleep, particularly the fever patients. There was strong resentment among the restless bachelors toward Liam O'Faoláin. He was like a scolding parent, always reminding them of what they should and shouldn't do, of rules and regulations and safety procedures. Cathleen understood why they resented him. She herself resented his heavy-handed authority. But she was also proud of his willingness to take on responsibilities when nobody else would. He didn't care what they thought of him personally as long as some order and discipline were maintained for the welfare of the group. A hard man he was, a strong man, and, in his own way, a good man.

Eventually he came to bed, the berth creaking as he lay down.

"Are you awake, Moira?"

"Yes. I'm uneasy tonight, that warm and restless. I can't feel comfortable."

"And Cathleen?"

"Long asleep, poor child."

He turned to his wife, whispered fiercely, "Almost grown, a young woman! I can't understand her at all. Do you know what she's done to us? The food is *gone*. We'll be paupers when we reach Quebec. Dependent on charity from strangers."

"Liam, she feels bad enough as it is. She was careless, and she's sorry for that. But guilt can leave scars. Don't make her suffer more than she already has."

"And what of the suffering she's caused the rest of us?"

"Go to sleep, dear. We'll manage."

Cathleen heard them touch, kiss, murmur briefly in the darkness. She was excluded, lost outside the tight, closed circle of their love. Always she had felt that way. One of her earliest memories was walking in sunlight down a road, holding her father's hand. Maybe she had felt security in his great presence, or perhaps he had said something kind. She only remembered the long, dusty road, the sunshine melting on her face, the joyful sense of belonging. She could not remember the last time he had touched her, or said an affectionate word.

Her parents slept. Cathleen lay, eyes wide open, watching the green spot of light at the open hatchway, where the ship's lantern burned all night. Her thoughts skipped over the sad events of the morning, and then those of the afternoon, and she thought of Jock Riordan. What kind of a boy was he? Like the other sailors, or the predatory first mate? No, he was just as he seemed, full of laughter and zesty, with strong feelings that well matched her own. *Excitable eyes, full of sparks,* what a bold thing for him to say. Yet the thought of him was the only thing that could comfort her. Wanting her to go on deck alone and meet with him in darkness! Why had he asked her to do such a thing? Because he knew that she would go! He knew her better than she thought.

There were snores and sighs all around her. Soon the child who dreamed of rats every night would cry out. Cathleen inched out of bed, pulling her shawl around her nightdress, moving cautiously. As she reached the ladder at the hatchway, a nightcapped head poked from the upper tier. "Hssst! Who's that?"

"Shhhh. It's me, Mrs. Roohan, Cathleen O'Faoláin. I can't sleep."

"I shouldn't wonder, you naughty child."

"I'm just going up for a breath of air."

"Better say some prayers while you're wandering about, then. Ask forgiveness. It was a terrible thing you did today. And, Cathleen . . . tell your mother I'll bring around what oatmeal I can spare in the morning."

Cathleen whispered her thanks, and the capped sentry

abruptly withdrew. She went on up the ladder and leaned her upper body out into the warm night air. A great floating stillness, an incredible calm. It was black, windless, without visible moon or stars. Lightning briefly lit the sky and she saw sails, ropes, spars, the mass of the forecastle sketched against the darkness. She waited, heard footsteps knock along the deck. Ready to duck down the hatchway, she breathed out, "Jock?"

"Cathleen!" She could almost hear the grin on his face. "Give me your hand."

Their fingers touched, joined. He pulled her along to the lee side of the forecastle. Then they stopped, leaned toward each other, straining to see in the darkness, laughing a little, both of them excited.

She whispered, "Are there others on deck?"

"The second mate's at the wheel. But he's deaf in one ear."

"I'd rather he were blind in one eye right now."

"If I can't see you, then he certainly can't." He pulled her close, tight against him. "I wasn't sure you'd come."

"I wanted to be with you. May I tell you something?"

"Anything. Recite the alphabet. Speak Hindi, if you like. But put your arms around me. Yes, like that."

"Five minutes ago I almost envied Minerva Flynn for being dead, I was that sad and alone. And now, because of you, I'm happy."

"Cathleen, what a grand girl you are." Then, his breath warm on her face, "Quick! Look up!"

A fantastic ball of light hung at the very top of the mainmast. Glowing, phosphorescent, it moved slowly downward, a wayward star.

"What is it?"

"Lord, it must be a corposant. Saint Elmo's fire, the sailors call it. It sometimes happens when the air is charged. They say you're lucky if you see it once in fifty passages." Unearthly, luminous, the light drifted slowly along the topgallant yardarm.

The fascination of it, the powerful feelings that linked their bodies, were a mystery to Cathleen, a stunning gift.

"By the powers," Jock whispered, as scattered drops touched down upon their faces, "here comes the rain. Give us a kiss, love." Then, laughing into the night, "Oh, what a lovely girl you are!"

17

As she reached the berth, her father's voice stabbed out of darkness. "Who's that?"

"It's me. Cathleen."

"What's the matter?"

"Nothing's the matter. I couldn't sleep. I went on deck for some air."

"Is there never an end to your foolishness? On deck, at this hour? You're never to go there alone at night!"

"Yes, Father."

She burrowed under the covers, and heard him lapse, still muttering, back into sleep. Thunder rumbled above. She lay awake for a long time, thinking of Jock, of kissing him, of the starry corposant. She thought of the universe, vast and orderly, stars and planets fixed and predictable. It was men and women who were all in confusion, and muddling along through it all was baffled Cathleen O'Faoláin on a voyage of her own, trying to discover her place in the scheme of things.

She was gliding down the edge of sleep when the storm exploded. The brig shipped a heavy sea, and water streamed down into steerage. Wind keened overhead as men struggled from their beds to close the hatchways. The child who dreamed of rats began to shriek wildly. Nobody could calm her.

"Cathleen?" Her mother's fingers gripped for her in the darkness.

"I'm awake."

"I'm going to need your help. My water has broken."

Mr. O'Faoláin sat upright. "The baby's coming *now*, this early? Are you in pain?"

"No, just uncomfortable. And soaked through."

Cathleen asked, "What shall I do?"

"In a while you'll have to wake Mrs. Hoult. Right now you'd best slip out of bed and find the parcel of clean cloths, and the baby things I've tucked away in the small chest. Liam, I want you to take Bartley—imagine, him sleeping like a lamb through this storm—and find another bed for him tonight. Perhaps the Roohans will take him in, there's only the two of them. And maybe we could pin some blankets up, for privacy."

Mrs. Russell complained from her upper berth, "What's going on? Are you trying to set us all on fire?"

"I'm lighting a lantern. My wife's in labor."

"A fine time she picked."

"As if I had any choice in the matter," Mrs. O'Faoláin whispered to Cathleen, as her husband hung the lantern on a nail at the back of the berth. He draped up quilts and blankets on both sides to form a makeshift cubicle, and then carried Bartley away. When he came back she said, "Thank you, Liam, dear. Now I want you to go and sleep with the single men."

"How do you expect me to sleep, Moira? I want to stay here with you."

"Please. I have Cathleen. She'll do what needs to be done."

109

"Then let me call in the surgeon."

"Him! Fiddle playing's more his line than delivering babies. No, Mrs. Hoult will come when it's time. Please, Liam, go. And good-night."

"You're sure Cathleen can manage?"

"Of course she can. We'll call you if you're needed." The brig tilted, sent him lurching backward down the center aisle. "Cathleen, I'll need some of those cloths here under my hips. That's a good girl. Now quick, blow out the candle, and get into bed with me."

In darkness again, Cathleen spoke. "I'm frightened."

"You needn't be. I'll tell you what's happening. Right now the muscles tighten up every few minutes, and that's to push the poor baby on its way, in case it changes its mind. Put your hand here and feel. It's a curious sensation, but not really painful. In the last stages only, that's when I'll probably cry out, but it's a natural thing to do, and you mustn't worry or mind, it's over soon enough."

During the next hour her mother's hand, holding Cathleen's, would gradually tighten and, after a few moments of pressure, would relax again. But Cathleen noticed that the spasms were closer together now, only a short time apart. And her mother's breathing had changed, become faster and rougher.

"What shall I do? Tell me quick what to do!"

"Light the candle again. And I think you'd best call Mrs. Hoult."

She was not a midwife, this fat, asthmatic, sleep-rumpled neighbor, but she had had eight children of her own, six still living, and she knew all there was to know about pregnancy and delivery. She had given birth to a set of twins, two breech babies, and a stillborn child. An hour after her last baby had arrived she had been up on her feet wanting to go to a wedding. Now, trying to yawn herself awake, she sat plumply on the edge of the bed and spread Mrs. O'Faoláin's knees apart to examine her. She had helped once before, when Eileen was born, but Cathleen had been sent away that time.

"The baby's coming quickly, there's no need to tell you that. You must work hard for me, dearie, when I tell you. But you've done it all before, the same as me."

For a while, there was only the steady military rattle of the rain, the sighs and movements of the sleeping passengers, and, stitched through these sounds, a deep and ragged breathing. Then a terrible cry was torn out of Moira O'Faoláin's throat. Cathleen had never heard anything so anguished.

"Mrs. Hoult, what's wrong!"

From the far end of the brig a man's drunken voice yelled out, "Shut her up, shut her up!"

"A poor soul's in labor," replied a woman indignantly. "Shut up yourself, you filthy brute."

"*Please*, Mrs. Hoult . . ."

"She's fine, Cathleen. Nature knows what to do, we only help out in a sensible way." She crooned, "That's it, dearie, now push down for me. Go ahead . . . ahhhhh, that's it . . . down . . . down . . . Alright, easy now . . . rest a little."

Under the lantern Mrs. O'Faoláin's face shone, wet and white. Her pale mouth was flattened, the deep-set eyes half-closed. Then she stiffened, braced her knees, and her breasts rose and fell as if she was struggling to lift a heavy weight.

Cathleen pleaded, "How can I help her, Mrs. Hoult?"

"Use common sense, Cathleen. Hand me some of those cloths there. You'd think, wouldn't you, with all the inventions nowadays, steamships and such wonders, that someone would devise . . . ah, that's it dearie, bear down again, good girl . . . something to help a poor woman in labor." Mrs. Hoult's breath whistled in her great chest. "But, no, there'd be no profit in that, it will never be done." She said quickly, "Come now, Mrs. O'Faoláin, it's almost over . . ."

"Hold on to me," Cathleen told her mother. "Pull as hard as you want if it will help." She braced herself on her knees in the berth, gripping her mother's hands as if they were involved in a desperate tug-of-war. The brig rocked violently, rain pounded heavily overhead, and there was a sharp crack of thunder. Cathleen was thrown down, and lost her hold on her mother. As the brig shuddered and tipped back in the opposite direction, there was a ringing clatter of falling pots and utensils.

Mrs. Hoult had applied pressure to Mrs. O'Faoláin's stomach. "Oh, the baby's coming, it's coming!"

Another lurch, the familiar shift of cargo in the center aisle, and the lantern, swinging on a hook, flickered and died. The candle was out and they were in total darkness.

"Dear God," Moira O'Faoláin panted. "What is it, what's happening?"

"Just a pocket of rough weather we're into." Cathleen frantically dug along the back of the berth for the hanging cannister of lucifer matches. "We've been through it before, so don't worry."

"Light the candle!" Mrs. Hoult sounded frightened.

"Please . . ." It was Mrs. O'Faoláin, struggling in her

effort. "Quick as you can . . . I'm afraid in the dark!"

Cathleen found the container, and steadied the lantern. There was a scratch, a rising pillar of light.

"Come now . . . oh, that's it, dearie. Ahhh . . ."

A baby girl slid out in a dark gush of blood, a glistening, tiny human parcel. Mrs. Hoult expertly picked her up, dangled her, shook loose a thin cry, then placed her on Mrs. O'Faoláin's naked belly. "Now, Cathleen . . . those little scissors I brought . . . if you'll just snip the cord."

"You think I can do it?"

"Yes," said her mother, "I want you to."

Cathleen took a quick breath. She was trembling with excitement. She snipped the umbilical cord, and Mrs. Hoult tied the navel with a piece of yarn. "Wipe the baby all over carefully, and dress her in the nightgown."

Cathleen dabbed at the little kicking legs, the moving arms, the hair still wet from birth. When the baby was dressed she wrapped it in a square of flannel and held the bundle against her body. The eyes were open, and small, shaken sounds came out of the tiny chest. "Such a little scrap, and doesn't she look cross!"

"And so would you," said Mrs. Hoult, taking away the stained cloths and putting fresh ones under Mrs. O'Faoláin's hips. "She didn't expect to be born in a place like this; it's enough to turn her sour for life. There, you've done a fine job with her . . . see . . . she has your fingers tight in hers already. Soon the afterbirth will come, and then the job is finished."

"Would you like some water?" Cathleen asked her mother when it was over.

"Oh, what I would give for a cup of hot tea," said

Moira O'Faoláin. "But, yes, a sip of water will have to do." And after she drank, "Whew! Pigs wouldn't drink this stuff out of a ditch."

"Tuck your new sister in beside your mother," said Mrs. Hoult, as Mr. O'Faoláin arrived and bent his shaggy black head to have a look.

"I heard the baby cry. It's over, then."

"Done. A fine wee girl. And your wife is as well as anyone could hope."

"Thank God for that." He touched the two faces in the berth. "Moira, sleep well."

"It isn't every newborn has a whole ship for its cradle." Mrs. Hoult yawned hugely. "And you should be very proud of your daughter, Mr. O'Faoláin."

"Yes, she's a fine, healthy baby."

"I mean Cathleen. A grand help she was, a grown woman couldn't have done better."

After Mrs. Hoult had climbed wearily back to bed, Moira O'Faoláin took a chill, a nervous reaction to the shock of giving birth. Cathleen covered her warmly with a shawl.

"Your hands are like ice, child."

"I wanted to help, but I was so frightened." Cathleen blew out the candle and got into bed. "Then, after a while, I wasn't frightened at all."

She was very tired. Around them the fussy creaking of the brig, swaying night sounds as the rain lashed down. Then, her mother's surprising laughter. "Isn't it funny," she said, "how men can sail around the world and bash themselves to bloody lumps in stupid wars and do all sorts of exciting things. But they miss out on the greatest adventure of all. It's a joke, isn't it?"

"I don't think it's a joke. I could never go through it."

"But you will, maybe many times over. And no matter what you saw or heard tonight, the truth is that the very best moments of my life have been just after a child was born. Like now. Sure, the worry comes soon enough, and all the fearful wondering if there'll be food enough . . . and nights when you hold a sick baby and hope it will still be with you at the sun's rising . . . and, yes, the squabbles and the strain when a child pulls one way and you want to go another."

"You've had your share of that with me."

"And the angry words that boil over and scald the child, words that should never be spilled at all. But that comes later, Cathleen. Much later." Her sleepy words fell soft against the pillow. "There's nothing better than that moment when a new life happens. Then everything is as fresh and hopeful and alive and kicking as the very first day of the world. That's God's holy truth, Cathleen. And men, poor dears, miss the best part of all."

18

"Say good morning to your new sister, Bartley."

"But I don't like her. She doesn't have a nose."

"Neither did you. At least, not much of one. But it grew on later, just the same."

It was early, barely light. The hatches were open; the grates on deck had been cleaned, the fires already kindled. Many of the adults still slept, while children played quietly in their berths.

"What's her name?" Bartley stuck his finger into the baby's mouth.

"Stop that now." His mother was only half-awake. "I don't know about a name. Maybe you have an idea."

"Call her Bessie. That was the cow's name, in Dublin."

"Bessie doesn't suit her at all."

"Well, I don't like her."

"You will, by and by."

Cathleen had awakened feeling much older. She thought again of Jock, of being kissed, of the corposant, of helping to deliver her own sister, all in one crowded night. She felt a new and certain bond with her mother, a sense of superiority over Liam O'Faoláin, who didn't really understand about childbirth at all. *You should be very proud of your daughter, a grand help she was, a grown woman couldn't have done better.*

Suddenly she sat up in bed. A spot of light traveled back and forth, circling, sometimes stopping. Bartley stared, intrigued. "What is it, Cathleen?"

"I don't know." They watched as the light flickered up and down and all around them. "Let's see if we can find where it's coming from."

They followed the floating beam back to where it spun and soared in butterfly flights from an upper berth. The Russell children giggled overhead.

"What's that you have up there?"

Mortimer Russell's shrunken face was splotched with measles. "Nothing." A smaller girl flung her head down over the side and crossed her eyes at them.

"Mirror," squealed out a smaller sister, who lay on her back, kicking her legs in the air. "We found it."

"Where did you find the mirror?"

Mrs. Russell's untidy head appeared, her hair sprawling loose from under a grimy nightcap. "What do you want?"

"Ask your children, please, if they'll show me the mirror."

"Why should they?"

"Because I lost one, and it might be mine."

"Say nothing at all to the nasty girl," advised their mother. "Waking people up at such an hour, just to cause trouble."

"I don't want to cause trouble. I only want to see what your children are playing with."

"Give it here." Mrs. Russell grabbed Mortimer's skinny arm and gave it a twist. An arc of light spun, flashed, and the mirror splintered on the planks below. "There! Satisfied, I hope!"

"No, I'm not." Cathleen knelt to scoop up the broken bits. "I think it might have been mine."

"We took it," chanted the smallest girl, "took it, took it."

Mrs. Russell exchanged this information with an angry cuff, and the child shrieked. Mr. O'Faoláin arrived and asked what all the noise was about.

Cathleen said, "If they took my mirror, they might have taken our food supplies as well."

"What mirror are you talking about?" he asked.

"Stole your food!" Mrs. Russell was screaming now. "The very idea. I ought to scratch your eyes out!"

"Nobody's accusing you of anything . . ." he began.

"*She* is! *She* did!" The widow scrambled down, red in the face, unlocked her own supply chest, flung back the lid. It was well filled with oatmeal, salt pork, potatoes.

"How could I possibly tell what does or does not belong to you, Mrs. Russell?"

"You can take my word for it!" she fumed. "A helpless woman all alone and see how she's treated. As a criminal, a common thief. And you, my girl, will be sorry for saying it."

Cathleen asked to speak to her father privately, and on the upper deck she told him about spending Aunt Wig's gift of money for the mirror in Dublin. "I'm sure the Russell children stole it and our food as well. But there's no way now of proving it."

He agreed. "I said strong words to you yesterday. But you must understand the hardship you've caused us."

"I'm sorry for it, Father, and I want to make it up to you. Miss Arnold wants me to take Minerva Flynn's place in the cabin. She's promised me good wages, and now we'll be able to buy supplies from Captain Greeley without using all our savings."

He was thoughtful for a moment, and she felt he was relieved. Then he said, "You know how scattered and forgetful you are, Cathleen. Do you think you can handle such a responsibility?"

"Yes, I do! I'm not a child, you know."

He seemed old, tired, resigned. "Then I think it would be sensible, Cathleen, for you to wait upon Miss Arnold."

"You've come back! Oh, I'm so glad. You've no idea how terrified I was during that storm last night. Look, I picked the stuffing out of the sofa."

"I'll help you poke it back in."

Elizabeth glanced around the cabin, gestured vaguely. "There won't be a great deal to do. Just a little tidying up and looking after my clothes and a bit of mending. That sort of thing. It's for companionship, really."

"Yes, Miss Arnold."

"And would you fasten my dress at the back, please. I couldn't reach the middle button this morning. Thank you." Elizabeth said, "I've been writing in my journal this morning. This voyage is the most exciting thing that's ever happened to me, and I want to remember it all. But I never thought I'd have to write about Minerva. I still can't believe she's gone." She turned away, tried to control her emotion, and when she was steadier she showed Cathleen her diary. "I've tried to describe how picturesque the emigrants look on deck . . . waiting at the fire grates, and the dancing and all."

Cathleen thought of the squalor in steerage, and wondered if the English girl would think that scene very picturesque. But she said nothing. The night they had watched over Minerva they had been equal partners in a tragic event. Now the relationship had changed, and she would respect that difference.

She settled down to her new duties, mended stockings, rinsed out underthings, made up the beds. These were things she had done, however clumsily, all her life. There was nothing difficult about them, and she tried to do them well. But Elizabeth paid little attention to such matters. What she needed most of all was a listener, and Cathleen had always been curious, eager to listen. She discovered that the intelligent girl who rummaged so fearlessly through her books, trying on theories and ideas like so many new clothes, was a complicated and unusual person, full of anxieties. Elizabeth was sick at the thought that she might see a rat or a cockroach, unaware that the Irish lived between decks on intimate terms with both. She was also terrified of lightning, thunder, and storms, frightened of sickness and disease. She worried constantly about her health. Her hands trembled, she suffered from headaches and stomach pains, she broke out in curious rashes, and had fits of sneezing. She dreamed in color, violent dreams that left her sweating and breathless. Aside from her health, she was only interested in her books and her Bible.

"Don't you ever pray, Cathleen?"

"No, Miss Arnold. Not any more."

"Why not?" Elizabeth studied the Scriptures for an hour each morning, and knew much of them from memory.

"Because I think of God as being English . . . as if He

were an absentee landlord, I suppose, like the one we had at home. Responsible, you see, and off somewhere looking splendid, but not quite interested."

"How can you think He's not interested?"

"What makes you think He is?"

Elizabeth asked, "How do you explain love and truth and beauty?"

"How do you explain famine and disease and poverty?"

"If you learned to pray again, Cathleen, I think you would find it a great comfort."

"I might find it a comfort, but would it ever change anything or help anyone?"

"Surely it would."

Expressing ideas that she had never spoken out loud to anyone before, Cathleen said, "I've never found prayers did a scrap of good. My father says it's because I don't pray for the right things. But I did pray for the right things. For people not to be badly treated, or hungry. That men shouldn't fight stupid wars, and women and children suffer on account of it. Those are right things. But praying for them is useless, it only gives us an excuse not to solve our predicaments."

"But to have no faith . . ."

"I have faith in myself." Cathleen was thoughtful. "Maybe I'm just practical, Miss Arnold. I know my opinions are different, but that doesn't necessarily make them wrong. I haven't been properly educated, so I've had to use my own brains and intuition to set my course. When my sister Eileen was buried—three years old she was and bright as a daffodil—Father McConaghy looked down at the poor mite and cheerfully told us it was God's will. What nonsense! That was a lie, and I told him so. No God would ever want a child to shrivel up with fever, and I said that anyone who submitted to that notion wasn't holy at all, only daft."

19

Mrs. Gogarty was first; the mother and father of two young children next; and then, a four-year-old boy: all, dead of the cholera that smoldered between decks. For many days a heavy rainfall battered the *Fair Western Lady*. Without fires there was no way to prepare hot meals or to warm drinks for the sick. Fear stalked the emigrants night and day. There was anger, too, for as the food supplies dwindled, the thievery increased.

Shut away in the passenger cabin, Cathleen felt uneasy in the calm. The crying, the quarrels, the drunken confusion were faint and far away, a distant, monotonous roar, like wind or sea. But every afternoon when Elizabeth rested and she returned to steerage to visit her family, it became all too real again. Cathleen carried with her an egg or an orange or any scraps she could salvage from the cabin meals. Once, on her way, she bumped into her father. He might have been her grandfather, he looked so gaunt and old. He said that he was going to try to see the captain. "But I doubt if he'll give me an interview. I think he'd like to see me wrapped in a sail with my feet weighted down, but I'll never give him that particular satisfaction."

"What's happened?"

"We've been cheated all along on the rations. I've

discovered that the ship's measure is a third less than a full gallon."

"Will there be trouble?"

"No. I couldn't get the Committee to come with me to complain. They're all afraid of what he'll do. So I'll go alone."

"I'll go with you!"

Surprised, he looked at her for a moment without saying anything. Then, "You'd better get along and see your mother. We miss you, Cathleen."

It was her turn to be set off-balance by the words gently spoken. He pushed past her and went down the companionway stairs.

Mrs. O'Faoláin hadn't been well since the birth of Mary Kate. There had been afterpains, and then she had suffered from a depression that was aggravated by the noise and the congestion. She was also worried about being able to keep up an adequate supply of breast milk. Bartley felt the lack of attention, since Mary Kate needed so much. He was jealous of the new baby, and now that his older sister had deserted him, there was nobody to laugh at him and he missed that. Irritable, miserable, he challenged all the little boys and most of the bigger ones to fistfights and wrestling matches. He sprained a thumb, swallowed a button, erupted with volcanic hiccups for two and a half days.

Everyone felt the boredom and monotony of the voyage. Somebody started a debating society, but the initial debate exploded into a free-for-all, with hair-pulling, name-calling, and some vigorous shin-kicking, and so the first meeting was adjourned as the last.

Women grew hot and jealous of their husbands, men were temperamental and suspicious of their wives. Card games turned hostile and ugly. Some of the men were heavily in debt, and desperate. Social drinking was an excuse for insults, combat, or oblivion.

"Liddy! How are you managing?"

"Well enough. I'm surprised you're still talking to me." A leaner, harder Liddy Dillon scratched herself absently for lice. "What with the gossip against me and all."

"I've heard nothing."

"Oh, the women are forever talking behind my back and shunning me to my face."

"Whatever for?"

"Because they're silly and evil-minded, that's why." Liddy nipped herself sharply below the ribs, pinched a louse between her fingers. "Anyway, I don't care about them."

"Do you have any food left?"

"There's no need to worry about me, I'm doing well enough," she said evasively. "So you've gone to work in the cabin. Lucky for you!"

"Yes, I can breathe there at least. And Miss Arnold is very kind."

"I have news, too. Young Timothy Healy thinks I'm a holy wonder and follows me everywhere. Lord, it's like having a black cat at my heels, gives me the shivers. So when things seem terrible bad I only think how much worse it would be if I were married to him."

They were laughing as the tall, brutal man who had frightened Cathleen early in the voyage moved toward them down the center aisle. Cathleen felt her knees begin to tremble, and a familiar sickness spread into her chest. He ignored her. Silently he held a hand out to Liddy. Without another word, or even a look at Cathleen, she followed him back into the shadowy depths of the steerage.

Bothered and indignant, Cathleen went along to see her mother. Moira O'Faoláin was propped up in bed, holding Mary Kate. The baby was awake, spreading her little fingers into a fan. She had wide eyes, the color of slate, and a ruffle of reddish hair. Cathleen picked her up and held her. "Where's that Bartley? Stopped his hiccuping, I hope."

"At last. He's off hiding somewhere. Mrs. Rourke just up and struck him this morning. Oh, we had words about it, I can tell you, and then she burst into fits of crying."

"Will you tell him that Miss Arnold wants him to come and visit her again? She really does enjoy his chatter. And she has a book about Pygmies that should occupy him for a while. Say, what's happening with Liddy Dillon? Strange company she keeps!"

Mrs. O'Faoláin avoided the subject. "Mr. Roohan's very bad, Cathleen. He coughs all night without stopping, and there's nothing anyone can do."

"I'm sorry for him. And more fever cases, too."

"I pray we'll be spared."

"Nobody will be spared unless we get some light and air down here, and people have hot food and drink."

"There's no help from the captain, he won't listen to any of us. Your father does what he can, but the men have turned against him and spend all their time gaming and drinking. The women, they're just as bad, picking at each other over trifles like a flock of silly chickens. And the Committee—if only they would insist that the steerage be scrubbed out now and then and the sick people separated from the rest. But, no, they'll not stand up to the captain, and so things get worse and worse. But I'm glad you're out of this mess and earning your own way."

Cathleen handed Mary Kate back to her mother. "She's so placid and content. Was I ever like that?"

"You?" Mrs. O'Faoláin laughed, the first time in days. "Why, you howled and raged. Dear knows the tantrums you put us through. I think the only thing that kept you alive that first year was your general indignation with the world you'd been born into."

Before she returned to the passenger cabin, Cathleen stood on the upper deck, staring out over the bulwarks. Everything appeared to be one shade, rain and sea merged into monotone, the color of grief. Her mother's words, a *general indignation*. Yes, and she felt it still as she thought of the horrors below. Ireland had been hard enough, and a lively scramble just to stay alive, without any expectation of anything more. But it had its beauties and its pleasures. Singing and joking, the pleasant running lilt of the language. This voyage was limbo, a gaping pause between two worlds, without law and order, unsweetened by any grace.

"Cathleen!"

Jock had come up behind her. She turned, saw his young face fresh with rain, the flash of his smile. Their hands touched, locked.

"Oh, I've missed seeing you," she said. "I've been attending Miss Arnold in the cabin, did you know?"

"Yes, and about the new sister as well."

"That Bartley—always popping, like grease on the griddle."

"I need the sight of you, Cathleen. I want to be alone with you, but I'm on the run. Will you come here tonight?"

"I can't. I promised Father that I wouldn't."

"I wish we could talk now. Think of me!"

"I do. And Jock . . ." She took hold of his arm. "Quick, let me see that tattoo."

He glanced around, and then, grinning, clenched and unclenched his fist. The movements made a red and purple mermaid, fat and bosomy, undulate upon his lower arm.

"Oh, get along with you." She laughed, and pushed him on his way.

Elizabeth lay on the sofa, her feet up, a folded cloth sprinkled with vinegar on her forehead.

"You can't imagine," she said, as Cathleen shook out her wet shawl, "how much I suffer."

Cathleen wanted to tell her how little she knew of real suffering, that only the width of a few planks separated her from scenes she could never imagine. She swallowed the words she had almost spoken and offered to read to Elizabeth.

"No, not now. Oh, I'm bored. Aren't you bored, Cathleen? Bored, bored!" she said. "Shall we talk?"

"If you like."

"Cathleen, are you ever jealous of me?"

The question was surprising. "No. Never."

"But don't you ever think that it's unfair that by an accident of birth I've inherited certain advantages?"

"Yes, I think about that. Life's a tangle of injustices, that's certain. But jealousy's a sick and feverish thing, Miss Arnold, and I've no use for it."

"Then I must tell you something about myself. I'm jealous, sometimes, of you."

"Me!"

"Here I am, all laid out like a funeral lily, and there you are, so wet and alive, with a tension and a bite and an appetite I'll never have." She sighed, added, "You've such good looks. I envy that."

"Oh, my." Cathleen sat down. "That's me? I didn't know I was like that. I think it pleases me, and yet . . . it could be a problem, couldn't it?"

"I don't see how."

"Because a person could be taken in, deceived. Think you were being bought by the yard, don't you see, when someone . . . a boy, perhaps, really only admired the fabric."

"Don't worry about it. Women *are* fabric, and never taken seriously."

"That's not fair, and I won't accept it."

"I knew you wouldn't." Elizabeth sat up, reached for the book beside her on the sofa. "I've been saving this for you. It's a radical tract called 'A Vindication of the Rights of Women,' and it's written by a woman named Mary Wollstonecraft."

"Radicals sometimes turn out to be right-thinking people who have been accidentally dumped into the wrong century. But a *woman* radical, what a rarity! Yes, I'd like to read her book."

20

Thirty-five days at sea. The *Fair Western Lady* becalmed, her listless sails flapping idly at the masts.

The sight, the sound of bodies splashing out of sight familiar now, a mildly interesting event. Mr. Roohan's cough was heard no more, and his gaunt widow paced the deck hour after hour, a marshal without a charge. The black-eyed youngest daughter of the Hoults, suddenly gone. A thirty-year-old spinster, who had sobbed and sung in her delirium, dead of fever.

Now there was the sight of the walking dead, emigrants who paced the deck with an invalid shuffle, wasted from hunger, dysentery, dehydration. Children who had swaggered like sailors early in the voyage had grown apathetic, yet surprisingly brutal at their games. Still the Irish crawled up from steerage, to cook their oatmeal, to suck fresh air into their cramped lungs, to stare ever and ever to the horizon for the first glimpse of land.

"Is there much illness in steerage, Cathleen?"

"Yes, Miss Arnold."

"But your family, are they all well?"

"Yes, all well."

"I'd like you to call me Elizabeth. After all, we're friends now." But Cathleen couldn't, not as long as she accepted wages. She lived a curious double life. Outwardly she was calm, companionable. Inwardly she burned with tension. She seldom talked about her own family, or the desperation of the Irish, because she was afraid it would seem as if she asked for something. The days in the cabin were long, hours spent in reading and talking while she mended stockings, looked after Elizabeth's wardrobe, and polished all the fine footwear. There were intense discussions; the English girl liked to skip from topic to topic—religion, politics, literature, the latest scientific discoveries, strange remedies for bizarre diseases. Thomas, bringing in trays, stood with his mouth hanging loose and rubbed his head in amazement at the flow of words. Then Elizabeth's nervous energy, without a focus, would suddenly collapse. Exhausted, she would lie flattened on the sofa, passive under vinegar water.

Afternoons they strolled upon the quarterdeck. The sea was still, like the warm, breathing flanks of a great animal. Cathleen was always on the lookout for Jock, and when she saw him their signals were secret and brief. A lifted hand, his hat tipped down over one eye, her smile tilting upward. Once he yelled her name loudly from the rigging, the word tumbling out over the Atlantic.

Elizabeth turned to Cathleen. "That sailor, did you hear him shout? It sounded like your name."

"Now, that's peculiar," said Cathleen.

She could never see enough of him. Sometimes, on her way to visit her parents, there would be a chance for a few words, but never, now, an opportunity to touch.

The strain of the voyage showed in spurts of violence and apathy among the emigrants. Gambling and drinking went on as before, punctuated by vicious fights, but no letters were read or exchanged, there was little laughter, fewer songs, and no dancing. It was rumored that the surgeon had gone out of his head from laudanum and been thrown into irons to prevent him from leaping into the sea. There was one powdery flash of excitement. An auction was held for the clothes of the dead spinster. Cathleen heard the cant as the items were put up for bid, thought how eerie it was that those skirts and petticoats would soon be animated on another owner. But this was novelty, a jagged break in the monotony, soon healed over.

Every day when she returned to steerage Cathleen brought what she could from the cabin. Sometimes a slice of mutton, a piece of cheese, or the brittle ship's bread. Elizabeth was often queasy, and at times wouldn't touch her food at all. Then, avoiding Thomas's pleading eyes, Cathleen would wrap the leftovers to take to her mother. She was ashamed of her own appetite. At mealtime she tried to eat as little as possible, to save what she could. But often the smell of the lobscouse, a stew made of biscuit and salt beef, or the Sunday duff was overpowering, and she would eat everything on her plate. Afterward she would feel guilty that she hadn't put more aside for her family. Her increased hunger was only one aspect of many changes she felt within herself. Her body had grown fuller, and strained uncomfortably against the tightness of her old dress. And her emotions were bewildering. One day she was irritable, and the next day anything could set her laughing. Nights were confusion. Then she experienced a different kind of hunger, which disturbed her mind and body, kept her sleepless. Jock was mixed up in it, and the need to see him and be with him.

One afternoon when she went below she noticed that Mary Kate was unusually restless. The baby drew up her legs and kicked them out again in jerky motions. She jammed a tight little fist at her mouth, again and again.

"What's the matter with her?"

"It's the lack of liquids. I don't have enough milk now to nurse her properly." Mrs. O'Faoláin rocked and jiggled the baby, trying to soothe her. "Cathleen, would you look in on your friend Liddy Dillon? There was a terrible argument last night amongst the women, and I've heard the girl was injured. Maybe there's something you can do for her."

"Poor Liddy, I will. Take care of yourself, Mother."

In the berth that Liddy shared with five other women a single figure lay covered with a ragged bedcover. Men and women stood nearby eating and gossiping, paying little attention to the groans of the sick or the crying of small children.

"Liddy." Cathleen shook the covers gently. A hand reached out and pulled down the quilt. Liddy's bruised and blackened face lay on the pillow, eyes swollen shut, her upper lip split and glued with dried blood. Her broken nose was flattened and disfigured.

"Liddy, what happened to you?"

"Och," came the voice, thick with pain and shock, "the women . . . sure, the women."

"But *why?*"

"You're such an innocent . . ." Was it a smile or a sneer? Cathleen couldn't tell. "Some of the men gave me food, that's all . . . and the women were angry about it."

"Who gave you such a beating?"

"No matter." Painfully Liddy turned her face away from the light. "It's survival, after all. It's a battlefield now, one against the other."

Cathleen spoke out to a group of women who stood watching. "Who gave this girl a beating?"

"Don't know," said one with thick, gingery hair, slackly chewing biscuit.

"Somebody must have seen it!"

"It's none of your affair."

"She's badly hurt. Don't any of you care?"

"Why should we?"

"Maybe now she's learned her lesson." This, fiercely spoken, from a middle-aged woman in a filthy dress whose hard face was cracked by deep wrinkles.

"Who taught her a lesson? And *why?* I want to know!"

"It was our men she was fooling with. Did she care if she stole food out of our mouths? She got what was coming to her."

Mrs. Russell's tight body and pinch-face emerged. She stared at Cathleen, chin up, spiteful and intense. "Liddy Dillon's a whore, a common, dirty whore!"

Cathleen felt raw with anger. "She's not!"

"Here's another troublemaker, ladies, come for some instruction. Abused my children, she did, and called me a thief to my face, and now she's come to defend that slut. Maybe she should have a taste of what the other one got."

Some of the women smiled, others were expressionless, but one by one they pressed in, enclosing Cathleen into a smaller and smaller space.

"Now, what was it you wanted, dear?" asked Mrs. Russell.

"I want to know who hurt Liddy Dillon!"

Amiable women, who had smiled and jigged and gaily waved good-bye to Dublin, now moved in, pressing tight against her, and Cathleen saw that they were capable of any violence. She was stripped down to an area inside herself that was brutal, passionate. If they struck, she would hit back. The sound of her own heart must be heard everywhere, like the noisy ship's pumps.

"Cathleen!" It was Bartley, crying out her name. "Let me through. Let me *through!*" He butted his head like a weapon all around the tight circle, kicking and pounding with his fists, jarring the women apart. Quickly they moved away, and it was over.

Captain Greeley stood talking to the soft-spoken second mate. As she passed them on the upper deck, she stopped suddenly. "Captain Greeley!"

He stared, astonished that she flung his name so boldly in his face, that she would dare to speak to him at all.

"A girl below is badly hurt. You must do something for her. And the conditions there . . . can't you see to it that the sick are kept separated from the well, that the steerage is scrubbed out? The fever and cholera have spread like wildfire. There's war going on down there, and you don't even care. Who'll buy your rum, Captain, when everyone is dead?"

The little second mate made frantic motions to Cathleen to be still. Calmly the captain polished the brass knuckles smoothly on his thigh.

"And why aren't there medicines on board? The surgeon's no more use than that figurehead. You used to have the bedding spread on Sunday, but once the prayers were stopped, you stopped the airing quick enough."

In a tightly coiled voice, the captain asked, "What's your name?"

"Cathleen O'Faoláin."

"Then tomorrow," he said, "when I give out half the water rations, the reason given will be Cathleen O'Faoláin. And the time after that, should you ever dare to speak to me again, the same reason will be given. And *again*. And *again*. It's a name, I think, your thirsty Irish will soon learn to hate."

21

"But why did you speak out?"

"I had to."

"Cathleen, that blistering tongue has kept you in trouble all your life. Now look what you've done. Every man, woman, and child in steerage must suffer on account of it. And today . . . half the water rations!"

Cathleen stood with her father at the foredeck. It was gray and sullen weather, the brig laboring at two knots an hour. She was conscious of the angry glances, the outspoken complaints against her.

"I'm sorry. Really sorry." How many times had she spoken these words in her lifetime?

"As Head of the Committee, it's my responsibility to speak for the rest, not yours. Captain Greeley has absolute power on this brig . . ."

She interrupted him. "I swear the power men have sometimes makes them crazy!"

". . . But we've learned best how to handle him. And we've had some concessions. Not many, I'll agree, but he's been fair about the recreation on deck. He's seldom interfered when dancing was requested."

"Because he made a profit from it!"

"That may be. But by attacking him you've only made it worse for the rest of us."

Cathleen said, "What I don't understand, then, is how

people deal with injustice. What you're telling me is that we must submit to it, yield to power or at best compromise. You don't ever want me to question authority, not yours, not the captain's. But I have to. How can I live the way you say I must?"

"See what happened when you spoke out in anger? Anger was returned."

"*You* always speak out."

"I'm a man. I have rights and the authority to protect those rights. You only have what I give you."

"It's human rights we're talking of, and you can't give me what is already mine. All of us have certain rights, but we'll have to fight for them. Listen, we are many, Father, and the captain and his crew are only a few. We can force him to give us what is ours."

"That's anarchy. Mutiny. The rule of the mob."

"No! It's justice!"

"Then for your own good leave justice to the men."

"You don't know what's good for me. You'll never accept me the way I am, will you?" She turned and walked away, ignoring the hostile stares of the emigrants. She was angry, confused, and upset. She wondered what it was that always compelled her to quarrel with situations others accepted. Liddy Dillon, for instance, beaten and ostracized below. She had thought of Liddy for such a long sleepless time in the night, shocked, and sorry, and, yes, curious too about that dark mysterious side of life nobody spoke about. The other women hated Liddy, but it was the conditions that had forced Liddy into such a bitter way of survival that Cathleen hated. She went below to see her.

Liddy lay in bed, staring at nothing, her face marked

with purple bruises. The broken nose blurred her jaunty profile. Cathleen had brought a pocketful of raisins for Bartley, but instead she offered them to her friend. The girl took them without thanks and stuffed them hungrily into her swollen mouth.

"Come below have you, to walk in our rubbish?"

"So you're angry with me, too."

"And why not? Making the captain cut our water rations. Not that it matters to you, living in luxury while the rest of us suffer. It didn't take you long, did it, to see which way the wind was blowing? You made up to the English lady and found yourself a soft and easy berth. I'd be ashamed, I would, to let my own flesh and blood rot here in steerage." She looked at her fingernails, pathetic little bits she'd chewed away. "Well, I'd like you to get a taste of what I got. You wouldn't be so stuck on yourself then."

Cathleen said nothing. She felt a sadness deep and intense, and she turned to go. Liddy reached out, tightly held on to her hand. "I'm sorry! I don't know why I said such rotten things, Cathleen. My head's confused. I don't trust anyone at all." She whispered, "It's not safe for me here anymore. They're waiting to get me, Cathleen. The women talk behind my back and plan against me. Last night a rat ran over me in bed. If it had touched my face I think I'd have died."

In the cabin Elizabeth tossed down her book, walked around the little space for a few minutes, and then sat on the sofa. She picked up her journal and flipped through the cream-colored pages. She showed it to Cathleen. Most of the pages were blank, or only contained a line or two. "Nothing. Day after day. I can't think of anything to write. Wind. Rain. Fog. One day mutton, another day beef. A treacle pudding—what a fascinating notation. In books I've read, sea voyages are terribly exciting. Pirates and mutinies . . . you know what I mean, things *happen*. But in reality, what could be more monotonous?"

Cathleen was very depressed. She thought of the drama seething below. Fever patients with heads grossly distorted, their bodies covered with black and festering sores; foul water covered with green scum; scant supplies; rank water closets. Mary Kate, frantic at the breast, fighting for survival. Liddy Dillon, selling herself for ship's biscuit. She liked and respected Elizabeth Arnold, but they were as separated by background and experience as if they'd been born and reared on different planets. Cathleen felt an eerie sense of isolation. She was banished from steerage, but in this tiny room she was not a legitimate occupant, only a spectator.

Elizabeth took out the tiny crystal glasses from the padded box inside her trunk. "Some wine, Cathleen?"

"No, thank you." People between decks were without water because she had spoken unwisely to the captain.

Thomas brought in dinner on a tray and set it on the little table. "Doctor Jones has roasted a chicken, Miss Arnold. It was me who had to kill it, and it ran all about with its head off. That was a sight, I can tell you. There's no smell as fine as the smell of a roasted chicken, unless it's a goose. Or a duck. Or a ham."

"You may have my dinner, Thomas," Cathleen said. "I'm not hungry for it."

She was quiet all evening, thinking of her family. She was worried about Mary Kate, and Bartley had looked so listless and pale. The words between her and her father still chafed and rubbed, opening old wounds. Elizabeth sat reading Wordsworth's poems aloud, and it seemed ridiculous to Cathleen, listening to romantic poetry when she could visualize the steerage at the same moment. She suggested that they take a walk on the quarterdeck.

They went up. The weather had cleared. It was a magnificent night. The ocean glowed with a strange phosphorescence, and the moon, a cold, hypnotic eye, stared brilliantly over the sea. The stars were close, dense, wild with light. The beauty of the night made Cathleen nervous and excited. She wanted to speak to Jock, she wanted to say his name, and, without intending it, she told Elizabeth about him.

"A sailor? On this ship? Has he spoken to you? He has! Where is he from? What do you really know about him?"

Cathleen said, "The only thing I know for sure is that I love him."

Elizabeth stood silent for a long time. "Take care, Cathleen. Love isn't a frivolous thing. It's a serious matter, a sacred obligation. I don't think it's wise for you to say that you love him."

"I have to say it. Because I feel it."

"How can you be sure that what you feel is love?"

"I can't pin another name to it."

Elizabeth asked, "Can you describe it to me? Is it a holy feeling?"

Cathleen laughed. How good it felt to laugh. "I don't know much about holy feelings. For me, it's like suddenly being rich. And unbalanced. A bit mad, really. Like walking a tightrope between laughter and tears. And then, sometimes, I feel as if I'm hopping barefoot on a peat fire."

Elizabeth didn't laugh. She seemed upset by this burst of information. "I'm sure the English would never describe it that way. From what I've read on the subject love is selfless and pure. You make it sound so . . . hot and acrobatic." She frowned. "Don't be misled, Cathleen. You're very young, and a man alone at sea might just amuse himself by saying superficial things, mightn't he? Without being serious, I mean."

"He might. But Jock's not that sort."

"He's a sailor. You must realize that when the voyage is over . . . I mean, you have to look forward to a time when . . ."

Cathleen cut through Elizabeth's well-intentioned words with her own, intensely spoken.

"Why must I look ahead? When I know it can only be bitter and dark. I know what I feel now, and I trust what I feel. If I live to be an old, old lady, all crumpled up and dried out and hardly able to gabble out my name, I'll still recall what I feel for Jock Riordan on this very night, and I'll remember it as love!"

22

A tangy, sunlit day. Cathleen, on her way down to steerage after several days away, heard whooping and shouting on deck. A young couple had just announced their plans to marry in Quebec and were being toasted and congratulated. It was a pleasant sound, the music and the laughter. Cathleen thought how fine it was that life could still be celebrated. Under the planks of the deck people had died, lay dying, would die.

There was a shout from the rigging. A sail was seen, a tiny scratch on the horizon. The effect was spontaneous, instantly cheering. Emigrants crowded onto the foredeck, talking with more excitement and animation than they had shown in days. Cathleen watched with them for a half hour, as hungry as the others for contact with the sister ship. Where was the brig from? Where was she going? She rose in their wake, coming strongly on, but Cathleen realized that it would be some time before they spoke her, and she went below.

"How long has he been this way?"

"Since this morning. He woke up with the vomiting and the diarrhea. Now it's cramps in his legs and feet."

Bartley lay in the berth, retching. Cathleen spoke quietly to him, chilled at the sight of his pallid skin. His fingers picked anxiously at the bedcovers. He had had a terrible dream, he told her, about the sea serpent, who came lashing across the blue thunder of the waves to get him. Eyes like green lanterns, a wicked red tongue, forked at the end. Steam popped and sputtered from the holes in his back. Bartley had tried to swim away, but an octopus wrapped its tentacles around his ankles and tried to suck him down, just as the serpent finally caught up with him and . . .

"And what, Bartley? Did the serpent really gulp you down then?"

"I think so. I woke up and was sick," he whispered. "Cathleen, Mrs. Rourke hit me."

"Oh, what a tale of woe it is. Now, I don't believe the sea serpent got you at all. What you did was tie a big knot in his tail, and then you rode him all the way to Canada. And Mrs. Rourke! That was a long time ago. Besides, you know how silly and nervous she is, and I'm sure she's very sorry."

"She liked hitting me. I could tell. She was glad she did it." He drew up his short legs under the covers. "I hurt. I *hurt.*"

Mrs. O'Faoláin handed Mary Kate over to Cathleen. The baby was damp and smelled sour; she battered her thumb around and around until it went into her mouth with a juicy sound. Cathleen said softly to her father, who had come to stand with them, "God in Heaven, it's the cholera Bartley has."

"Yes. The others started just this way."

"Mr. O'Faoláin?" Young Mrs. Rourke clutched at his arm. "I must have a word with you." She drew him along the center aisle, then stopped and began to cry, wiping at her eyes with small, pink hands. "I didn't mean to strike the lad, that time before. He kept whirling around me, and I asked him please to stop it, but on he went, faster and faster, and I'm a very nervous and sensitive person, Mr. O'Faoláin, and all of a sudden I struck him. And now he's sick, and I'm as sorry as can be. He's really a good little fellow, I'm sure, and as bright as a new coin. Tell him, please, that Mrs. Rourke is sorry."

"I'll tell him. And he'll be up and teasing you again in no time at all."

"But it's the cholera, isn't it? The *cholera*, Mr. O'Faoláin!"

"Ma wants you. Ma says you have to come and help." Grubby hands pinched Mr. O'Faoláin's sleeve. It was one of Mrs. Russell's ghostly children, all so haunted and undersized that Cathleen could seldom sort out one from another. "Morty's finger is stuck in a hole. He was spying on the men and got his finger jammed, and we can't pull him out."

Cathleen followed her father back to the stern. Mortimer Russell had poked his finger through a knothole in the partition and was stuck fast. His finger was badly swollen, and every time he wriggled it he swore louder than before.

"Stop that filthy language now. How did you get stuck in the first place?"

"Trying to make a bigger peephole."

"Keep still, and I'll set it free." Mr. O'Faoláin tried to wiggle the finger loose, but it was too swollen. He took out his pocketknife.

"Ma! He's going to cut me finger off!"

"Look here, boy, I'm only going to whittle you loose." He steadied Morty's hand and delicately worked the blade of the knife into the edge of the knothole. After a few seconds the finger slipped out.

"Look at that! Like a sausage! And it hurts like the very devil, too!" Morty stared ferociously at Mr. O'Faoláin. "You might have cut it off, with a slip of the knife."

"Better watch your nasty tongue, then. I could still get careless."

Mrs. Russell sidled up, working her features around into whatever she used for a smile. "Don't be rude, Morty. And thank Mr. O'Faoláin for his trouble." Then she said, "I know that your boy is taken very bad, and I hope that when the time comes you'll remember I've a large family, and you've no other sons, so that when it comes to the disposal of the clothes . . . well, you can see that Morty here needs shoes and trousers and shirts and such. I only wanted to put in a word first thing, so that you'll remember a helpless widow and not give things away to them that already has them."

Cathleen rocked Mary Kate so violently that the baby burst out crying, but her father said calmly that in the event Bartley's clothing should have to be disposed of, he would give Mrs. Russell every consideration.

"Och! The very nerve," Cathleen said, when the woman was out of hearing. "I'd have let Morty hang on the wall until doomsday, I would. And now she's burying Bartley on us, and you let her!"

"Enough, Cathleen." They walked back toward their berth. "She's only a poor, vulgar woman, all alone in the world with five dependent children. She did what she felt she had to do. Let's hear no more about it."

"Let me stay and help nurse Bartley."

"No, you've a job to attend to in the cabin."

146

"But I feel so useless there, and lonesome for you all. I'm afraid for Bartley, Father."

"I know you are. But I'm not letting him go." Cathleen saw that he was a man without resources, backed against a solid wall of despair, but he repeated the stubborn words. "I'm not letting him go. So get along now. Miss Arnold will be wanting you back. We need the wages, Cathleen."

"Then send for me, if there's any change with Bartley."

There was great excitement on deck. The brig that had been gaining on them all afternoon was very near, and soon it drew alongside. The seas had risen. Fresh wind pounded the sails and hurled spray high over the decks of both vessels. The Irish pressed against the bulwarks saw a mirror image of themselves on the foredeck of the other brig. They waved, shouting to one another, but the rough wind snatched the words away. Captain Greeley shouted through his speaking trumpet. The other captain shouted back, but nobody could understand what he said.

The first mate brought up a large board, blocked out FAIR WESTERN LADY on it, added DUBLIN, and held it up in the air. As the emigrants watched and waited a similar message was printed on the other brig and held for them to see. FITZROY was written, and CORK. Another word was quickly added: CHOLERA. Captain Greeley stared at the message, but he did not respond. He made a jerky signal of departure, and the two boats eased apart. There was no other way to communicate, and there was nothing left to say. Cathleen saw that many of the emigrants were crying. It had all been disappointing and unsatisfying.

Tim Healy, standing behind Liddy Dillon like a spare shadow, came over to talk to Cathleen. "Another shark's been after us all day, have you noticed? I wonder who'll be next."

23

Elizabeth wore a beautiful dove gray dress, with fine lace frosted along the neck and the drifting edges of her sleeves. There were still the fresh marks of a comb in her neatly arranged hair. Her journal lay open in her lap, and on the little table beside her was a tea tray, with a china pot and stacked cups. She looked clean, comfortable, content.

"Cathleen, the most amazing thing! The captain's yellow bird has been singing all the afternoon, and you know he never sings. Thomas says it's because the bird smells land. Do you suppose that's possible? I can't smell anything, can you?" She went on, "Anyway, I've written it all up in my journal. It makes an interesting event, at any rate. And there's been so little to record." She snapped the diary shut. "It's been mostly blank pages since Minerva died."

"Then I'll give you another item." The words were flat, bitter. "My brother has cholera."

Elizabeth sat, her eyes large with shock. "Oh, I'm so sorry. And he's very ill?"

"Yes."

"Then let me go and see him."

"No, you mustn't do that."

"Why not?"

"You can't expose yourself to it."

"We nursed Minerva, and nothing happened to us. I want to see him, Cathleen. Perhaps there's something I can do."

"There's nothing anyone can do."

"I want him to know that I care about him. Only for a few minutes, Cathleen. You can't object to that."

Cathleen's hands were sweating. "What you've seen of us from the quarterdeck," she said, "may have looked very quaint, with our shawls and our kettles and jigs. In fact, you've said so." She drew a deep breath. "But in steerage, Miss Arnold, it's not a pretty picture at all. It's not healthy. I'm afraid that it might make you sick." She softened the rush of words. "I haven't told you much about it because I didn't think it was your concern. But I don't want you to go down there."

"Bartley's my concern. Other than you he's the only friend I have on this boat. And I *will* see him. Now what can I take to him?"

Cathleen saw that there was no point in arguing about it; Elizabeth Arnold had made up her mind.

"We're very short of water."

"But it's disgusting. Who could drink it?"

How many times had Elizabeth, with her own plentiful supply of expensive wine, splashed a day's allotment of water on her face and hands without even thinking about it? Cathleen said, "We're desperately short. I think it would help if you could spare a little."

She had, in time, grown used to the clamor between decks, the muddled combination of crying, groaning, and rambling gossip, the rowdy children, shrill women, drunken men. But as she led the way down the ladder, with Elizabeth only a few steps behind, Cathleen saw and heard it all for the first time, as the English girl must be experiencing it. Water slopped down through the open hatchway. Below, it was dim, stagnant, smoky. In the berth closest to the ladder lay a woman, her head bloated beyond recognition, in the last stages of the fever. Cathleen looked over her shoulder at Elizabeth. The young girl's face was dazed with shock and revulsion.

"Watch your step, Miss Arnold."

Around them expressionless faces. Only the eyes of the children held any real curiosity about the English lady.

"Here's a visitor come to see you, Bartley."

Mrs. O'Faoláin thanked Elizabeth for the water. Her face was creased with worry and strain. "It was kind of you, indeed it was, Miss Arnold," she said. "He's taken very bad, as you can see. He's never been quiet five minutes in his life, and look at him now."

The boy in the bed was shrunken, foreign, his skin lax and clammy, the eyes sunk into deep, bluish pockets. He recognized Elizabeth and anxiously stared at her, as if he expected to be told bad news.

She sat on the blanket and took hold of his hand. "Bartley, do you remember Harvey, the captain's goldfinch? Well, he's been singing this afternoon, and the steward says it's because he smells land. And that must mean that the voyage is almost over. Soon we'll be in the Gulf. Now," she said, "you must get well at once, because soon we'll see the ice, and I've read what a spectacle that is, like floating castles." She had brought him an orange, and she put it into his hand and fastened his fingers around it. "This will make you feel better. There's sunshine in it, all sealed up inside. You think about that."

Bartley looked at the orange, and Cathleen could imagine him thinking of a warm blob of sunshine melted in it, waiting to be swallowed. Elizabeth stayed only for a few more minutes. When Mr. O'Faoláin came by, carrying Mary Kate, she praised the baby, said good-bye, and then hurried to the upper deck where she was immediately sick, over the side.

"I asked you not to go below."

Elizabeth mopped at her damp forehead with the lace edges of her sleeves. "I should have gone there sooner! How ridiculous I must have seemed to you all this while . . . how insensitive and foolish sitting on that stupid sofa . . . deaf and dumb and blind. Such human suffering . . ." She choked on the words, and turned her face away. "You must feel great contempt for me."

"But I don't. It has nothing to do with you."

Elizabeth faced her angrily. "You're at fault, for keeping me in ignorance. And you wrong me by thinking that I wouldn't care. I know that I'm trivial and silly, but I'm not callous, Cathleen. How could I not care?"

"There's nothing you can do."

"Isn't there? Don't be so sure about that. I can write, and I *shall* write to whatever authorities are responsible for allowing conditions like that to exist. Threaten, I can do that, too. I can even learn to swear, if I must, if that's how I have to communicate with the captain in order to have that hole cleaned up." Excited, she lurched back and forth with the roll of the brig, tripping over cordage.

The first mate stopped. "You'd better go to the cabin, Miss Arnold. Weather's too rough now for strolling about." He smiled, the wide cave of his mouth showing a few blackened stumps of teeth. As he moved along he gave Cathleen a hard and intimate pinch at the back of her waist. She gave him a furious shove.

"Here now, what's that for?"

"Keep your hands to yourself."

"I never touched you."

"I say you did. You're always handling the women on the sly."

"And who'll believe you?"

Elizabeth Arnold said, "I believe her. And you'd better believe me when I tell you that I'll report you to the captain."

24

In all their hope and ignorance, many of the Irish thought that approaching the Gulf of St. Lawrence meant an end to their misery, and that the conclusion of the voyage must be only a few hours away. The shout of "Land," even without the sight of it, stirred them wildly, all except those who were too sick to believe they would ever see it again. The word was repeated over and over during the afternoon as they swarmed up from the belly of the ship to stand, to sniff, to stare. Some, in an innocence of longitudes and latitudes, were already dressed in the best clothing they owned, special linens, laces and ribbons saved for display, to dazzle the Quebecois.

Yet from the deck on this bright morning they saw the same heaving blanket of the Atlantic which had flapped for weeks before their eyes. But there were small discovered differences. A swallow, wing-weary, resting in the rigging. Flying insects riding on a land breeze. And the first shape of ice, hunched on the level branch of the horizon like a gigantic frozen bird.

Mrs. O'Faoláin was not among those on deck. Bartley had gone into an alarming decline. She sat with him, unable to feel his pulse, wanting to breathe life into him. She had lost one child; it wouldn't get easier with repetition. And what of Mary Kate, fighting for milk that was inadequate?

Cathleen came down into steerage, stood beside her. She put an armload of bottles on the blanket, whispered, "It's Madeira wine. Miss Arnold says you must drink it, that it will be good for you and help the baby." She bent to look at Bartley. "How is he?"

"See for yourself. Can you stay with me for a little while?"

"Yes. Miss Arnold has gone off to see the captain. She's in a great storm over what she saw here yesterday."

"Thank her for the wine, Cathleen. It goes to show that there's good in everyone, doesn't it? Even the English."

Cathleen put her lips close to Bartley's ear. "Do you remember what Miss Arnold said about the yellow bird? Well, it's true. Harvey's almost blown his head off singing, and everyone on deck has been wearing out his eyes for a sight of Newfoundland. And cold—like a breath of winter. Bartley, I've seen three great chunks of ice, you wouldn't believe the size, and one all covered with birds, thousands of them. The captain has just sounded, to see how deep the water is, because the men have been pestering him to let them fish. And wouldn't a taste of cod be fine?"

She described the sounding procedure: the sails set back, a seaman at the stern holding a reel while a line was uncoiled and drawn along outside the ropes of the rigging to the bow; the lead attached, carried to the point of the bowsprit where Jock (joking, as usual) waited for the order from Captain Greeley; Jock heaving the lead! It plummeted with a solid splash, and bottom was found at fifty fathoms. When the lead was drawn up it was filled with fine, light sand. She didn't tell Bartley there had been time for a few words with Jock.

"Where's Bartley? I never expected him to miss this."

"He has the cholera," she said. "Oh, Jock, so many have died of it."

His face, without the boy's smile, was strangely adult. "Look, Bartley's the sort of a kettle who never boils dry. Not for another hundred years at least. He'll be alright. Tell him I said so."

She felt better at once, sure that he must be right. Now, looking at her brother, she lost confidence and was afraid again. Bartley's eyes were closed, his face the color of skimmed milk. She wondered if he had heard anything she'd said. The wailing of children, the moans of the sick, the smell of despair overwhelmed her. She had to get out into fresh air again.

On deck sailors were already fishing, properly equipped with hooks and lines. The Irish, in the scramble to begin, improvised with twine or thread, padlocks and bolts, their lines snarled and tangled in the rush. Then there were shouts and cheers as the first thumping codfish, mackerel, and halibut were hauled over the side.

Fresh fish! They flashed and slid across the deck. Women ran for their frying pans, stirred up the coals, jostled for a place at the grates. As fast as the fish were caught, quick hands seized, split, and cleaned them. The raw chunks sizzled in smoking pans; children ran, shoving cod into their mouths, spitting out bones, shouting for more. The smell saturated the chilly air. The Irish had felt they would never be carefree again, but this was a festival—they were suddenly happy and knew it.

The surgeon, released from irons, came on deck, blinking wanly into the sunlight, his fiddle under his arm. For an hour he played, lacing the air with skeins of melody, but everyone ignored him. He had failed them when they most needed him, and not a tune that he could play would ever seduce back their dead.

"Cathleen, look what I've caught!"

Jock's brown face split white with smiling, and his arms wrapped around an enormous, staring codfish. "He must weigh twenty pounds at least. Would you like him?"

"I'll give him to Father. Thank you, Jock, he'll last forever."

There were so many people crowded about them, and so much activity, that she felt it was safe to snatch a few minutes conversation with him. "Is the worst of the voyage really over?"

"The ice is always a menace, and there's a real danger of fog. And near Anticosti the sunken reefs as well. So it's not over yet."

"And when we reach Quebec, then what will happen?"

"You'll go on to Montreal, and then to York."

"I mean, what will you do?"

"Oh, another voyage. Do you know what I'd like? To ship out on a New England whaler someday. Maybe see the coast of California. There's no chance of that now. This time it will be a timber ship back across the Atlantic." He grinned down at her. "But it's a grand life, Cathleen. It really is. Hard and dirty, but I'm used to that. It's the freedom I enjoy, and the places I've been,

and the people I've met. Oh, brawls and the like . . ."
He laughed, eyes keen with remembering. "Tales that
would stand your hair on end. If only we had had the
time to really talk, to get acquainted."

She stood abandoned in the face of his open good
spirits.

"You're very casual, aren't you? After Quebec, then,
it's just farewell and over, all the good feelings between
us." She remembered what Elizabeth had said about
young men at sea, and stood holding the giant codfish like
an awkward dancing partner, thinking it was true.

"Farewell for sure. But the good feelings, they'll not be
soon forgotten."

Captain Greeley advanced along the deck with a scowl
on his face.

"Then you were only larking with me after all."

Sweat popped out on his forehead, in spite of the cold.
"You're a very young girl, Cathleen. And I have to make
my own place." They both saw that the captain had seen
them together. "Look, I don't like this sort of chat, we'll
both say stupid things we'll be sorry for."

"I'm not sorry for anything I've said. All this time I
thought you were caring."

"And I thought you were such a special one, not
expecting promises and declarations. Independent, like
me!"

A shout went up from the foredeck. "Land!"

More than a sniff of it this time. The actual sight.
Forty-two days at sea. Gloomy Tim Healy had won the
bet.

25

"And then what did the captain say?"

"He said he couldn't understand what I was complaining about, and hadn't I been given everything I'd paid for?" Elizabeth walked the cabin floor, first playing herself, and then buttoned up into the role of Captain Greeley. " 'Yes,' I said to him, 'that's quite true, I'm as comfortable as I expected to be, but that's not the problem.' "

Elizabeth paced the other way, her voice harsh and dry. " 'Then what is the problem?' he asked me, looking as if all he wanted was for me to leave him alone so that he could get on with really important matters.

" 'It's the emigrants,' I told him. 'I want you to know that I've been into steerage, and conditions there are deplorable. I'm shocked,' I said, 'that you would ever allow such unbelievable filth and disorder on your brig, with no comfort for the sick. I'm sure that I saw a dead body, and who knows how long it's been there?'

" 'Well, what do you expect me to do about it?' he shouted, and went into a great tirade against the shiftless Irish, and said they were better off on his boat than starving at home, and that he obeyed the Rules and Regulations Act to the letter and so on. I cut him off short and told him not to bother explaining what a fine fellow he was to me, he could explain it all to the authorities when they investigated my report.

" 'My father's a retired naval officer, and knows important people,' I said, 'and he'll direct me to those who are in charge.' "

"Then what did he say?"

"Not much. He looked as if he'd like to give me a crack on the skull with those brutal little knuckles he's so fond of polishing, and I told him that if he was wise he would do something about cleaning up the mess and helping with the sick and burying the dead, and I used a lot of fine words to boggle him, and then I stamped out of there. But I will do it, Cathleen. I will write a report, and I will demand an investigation. If Captain Greeley gets away with such neglect of his passengers, then so will others. And this is no time for prayers, it's action that's needed. Except for Bartley. Prayers are all I can do for him. And I want you to stay with him tonight. I can manage on my own."

All night the foghorn sounded, rude and ominous. Cathleen sat with Bartley, awake while her mother dozed, napping herself when her father took up the watch. Mary Kate was passed back and forth among them, and never woke at all. Inside the lantern the candle burned, a smear of yellow rubbed on darkness as the slow hours dripped away.

Soon it would be morning. Cathleen had persuaded her mother to lie down and try to sleep. Her father had gone to walk on the upper deck. She held Bartley's hand, thinking that this voyage had been his only chance for a decent life. How cruel it would be to have it snatched away when they were almost within reach of the new land. She thought of Elizabeth's faith, and knew that she herself had none. There was no way she could bargain for her brother's life, her prayers would be dishonest. But she argued for him anyway, silently insisting that he had a right to see his new home, to help break ground, to grow up in his wild and joyful way. There was only one like Bartley, and he mustn't die. Her father had said that he wouldn't let him go, and she had believed him. Yet looking at her brother, masked by cholera, she was very frightened. She tried not to think of what might happen to Bartley. Instead she thought of Jock, going over and over in her mind the things she had said to him.

Forward, that's what her father always said she was, and that's what she'd been. But she'd had no experience with attractive young men, nothing to guide her but her own feelings. And a lot of help they had been, pushing her straight into his arms at the outset, keeping her jangled for weeks. What had she expected of him? She didn't even know how to answer that. She only hoped he wasn't laughing at her, thinking what a fool she had made of herself, asking him to put into words what he never once intended.

Elizabeth would understand. At least *she* wouldn't laugh. Cathleen thought of how strong Elizabeth had suddenly grown, all her energies focused on battering Captain Greeley into submission. She had wealth, education, and position, and it gave her the leverage none of the Irish possessed.

"How is he?" Shaggy, unshaven, her father was back.

"About the same."

"We were fools," he said. "Dreaming, that's all it was,

to think that leaving Ireland would make things better. If he dies, I'm to blame."

Something had happened to her father. This was a tired, defeated, strangely shrunken man.

"Stop it," she said. "You're worn out, and no wonder, but as for dying and blaming and all that nonsense, I don't want to hear about it. Why don't you lie down for a little, just close your eyes."

He didn't argue. "I *am* tired. Tired down to my bones."

She had never in her lifetime heard him admit it. "Then rest."

He looked at Bartley, and lay down on the berth, with an arm flung over his face. He'd given up, it was plain to see. Never again would he loom so large. Strange that she should love him more now than ever before.

"What's that noise?" Bartley asked.

She had drifted off, still sitting up. "Bartley, are you alright?"

"I dreamed of ice."

She whispered, "It's all around us. And that noise is a foghorn. It's very thick out there, and as cold as can be." She could feel the tick of his pulse now, and in the early morning light see the cyanosis fading from his skin. "That horn warns fishing boats that we're here, so they won't bump into us." Excited, she called to her mother, who slept cradling Mary Kate. "Wake Father too! Bartley's better, I can see that he is!"

They crowded around him, peering into his face, all talking to him at once.

"Are you thirsty?" asked his mother. "Miss Arnold

sent me some juice squeezed out of oranges especially for you."

Cathleen helped raise him, feeling the scrawny bones prick through his nightshirt. "There. Better?" Hugged him.

"Mmmmmm," he said. "I don't want to be dumped into the sea."

"Not you, Bartley. Jock says you'll live another hundred years."

"May I get up? I want to see the ice."

"No, you rest now," said his father. "Stop the chattering." Bartley shut his eyes. He slept.

As Cathleen was leaving for Elizabeth's cabin, her mother turned from nursing Mary Kate. "The milk is flowing again. Maybe it was the wine, and I thank God for it, but I think it's the pure relief over Bartley." Cathleen put her arms around her, and, squeezed between them, the baby made a small satisfied sound.

The morning smoked. Mist clung to the sails and shrouds, and Cathleen could barely see more than a few steps ahead. She was uneasy, aware of the menace of the ice floes stacked around them. Someone bumped into her. It was the gentle, apologetic second mate, soon lost again in the fog.

She went down the companionway stairs, thinking that she felt peculiar. She had developed a bad cold, her throat ached, and in spite of the penetrating chill of the Bank weather, her face was hot and dry. In the passenger cabin she found Elizabeth still asleep, buried under a mound of bedcovers.

Cathleen sat down on the red velvet sofa and suddenly

began to cry. From the great relief over Bartley, and being exhausted, for Liddy's battered face, and from being shunned by friends and neighbors. She cried for Jock, who would soon find another voyage and enchant another ignorant girl. After that she cried because she missed Ireland. It had given her nothing much, except the size and shape of her identity, but that was enough after all. A barren place for the O'Faoláins, but, oh, remembered mists and bogs, the smell of peat, the softness of the air, the sweet sadness of songs they had sung. And Aunt Wig's yeasty laughter rising through the years. She cried for Liam O'Faoláin because she loved him, and because he would never understand her in a thousand years, and for Minerva Flynn, speckled and shy, who had died too soon. There was so much to cry over, and be sorry for, and then she thought again of Jock, and her standing on deck holding that enormous, staring cod, wanting love words in the middle of a fish fry. She laughed. Laughed so hard and so long that Elizabeth woke up, as startled as if the world had rocked suddenly to a stop. "Whatever is it, Cathleen?"

"Bartley will soon be well again."

"Then praise God for that!" And Elizabeth did, fervently and in her nightgown, embroidering her prayers with many "thees" and "thous" and "therefores" and, after all of that, a ringing "Amen!"

26

A crash and thump in the outer passageway. A body lay at the bottom of the companionway stairs.

"He'll have broken his neck, whoever it is," said Elizabeth.

Cathleen knelt beside the sprawl of arms and legs. "But I don't think he's broken at all, or even bent very much. It's that Timothy Healy, who won a gallon of rum yesterday. Look, his arms are still tight around the jug, and it's not broken either."

"I can smell the drink from here."

"We can't leave him for the captain to trip over."

"Then let's drag him into the cabin until he gets his wits pieced together."

They each took hold of a leg and dragged him down the corridor and into the compartment. Tim's clothing was rumpled and torn, his face flushed, and he had a piece of red rag tied around his forehead.

"Where do you suppose he got that? It looks like that bit of cloth the cook wears."

"Thomas says Doctor Jones wears it to protect him from disease," said Elizabeth. "Like an amulet."

"He'd slit Tim's throat to get it back. I've never seen him without it."

They propped the body up against the sofa. With his

165

arms still wrapped around the gallon of rum, he opened his eyes and smiled. "How did I get here?"

"You must have fallen down the stairs, so we dragged you in. How do you feel?"

Tim heaved himself into a sit, and uncorked the jug with a vibrant pop. "Truth is . . . never . . . felt better." He took a large swallow from the bottle. *"Wonderful* stuff." He hugged the rum. Then he smiled at Cathleen. "You're beautiful." His head and hands flopped strangely. Politely he turned to Elizabeth. "And *you're* beautiful. I've never been this happy before. I have no parents, you see, and I've been kicked around and knocked about all my life. But today I'm happy." He giggled. "Nicknamed 'the Shadow' I was, because they said I cast a pall on things. Oh, very welcome at wakes, and much in demand as a pallbearer. It's my disposition to be grave." This remark sent him into a fit of laughter. "Did you get that? To be *grave,* I said, right after telling you that I was popular at wakes—do you see the fun in that?" He took another swallow of rum. "And now the parish is sending me out to a frozen white country full of wild animals, where I'll likely be knocked about and kicked around some more. But today . . . I'm happy." He said to Cathleen, "You don't look happy."

"I don't feel very well, Tim. I'm coming down with a cold."

"Then have some of this. Perk you right up again. A sure cure for what ails you. Look what it's done for me!" He sloshed the bottle around. "Cure for seasickness, cure for sadness, it must be a cure for the common cold."

"Might it help?" Cathleen asked Elizabeth.

"I've no experience with it. My father claimed it helped his heart, and my old aunt always swore it stopped her rumbling and helped her digestion."

"Works wonders," Tim said with a grin.

"I suppose the trick is knowing how much is the proper dose. It's obvious you've had too much."

"How can I have had too much when I feel this well?"

"I feel so miserable I don't suppose it would hurt to try a little." Cathleen poured out half a tumblerful. After the first hot swallow she made a face. "Och, that's foul!" It felt as if a red-hot poker had been rammed down her throat.

"It's only the first drink pokes up the fire," said Tim, now an authority. "The second spreads it around a bit."

Cathleen took another gulp. "It's a punishment for sure. How much would you say was a moderate dose?"

"My aunt took three little glassfuls before dinner," Elizabeth said, "and then sang all the way to the table."

"The more you take," advised the Shadow with confidence, "the better you feel."

The fire in the pit of Cathleen's stomach had mellowed and flickered out into the farthest reaches of her body. Fingers and toes, which hadn't thawed in weeks, felt warm, tingled. Tim Healy began to sing loudly and badly, thumping on his thighs and pounding his feet, all out of rhythm. Cathleen poured another tumblerful of rum and drank it down. She did feel better. All the things she had cried over now seemed far away and unimportant.

"We'd better muffle him up," said Elizabeth, "before the captain thinks someone is being murdered."

"Maybe some fresh air would help." Cathleen clapped Tim on the shoulder and gave him a shake. "Come on, old boy. We'll take you for a walk."

He was perfectly willing to go, it was his legs which were so disagreeable. Cathleen pulled from above while Elizabeth panted and shoved from below. They yanked him up the companionway stairs and propped him on deck against the bulwarks. Cathleen couldn't stop laughing, and Tim wouldn't stop singing about a buxom young maiden from Galway, who lured gentlemen into a hallway. Over and over again the foghorn sounded, as sailors appeared and vanished in the flow of fog.

Jock appeared out of nowhere, amazed. "What the devil's going on here? I never heard such a racket."

"We're taking a walk," Cathleen told him.

"In this cold weather?" He looked closely at Tim. "Can't you see that this lad is drunk?"

"Happy," Cathleen insisted. "We're all happy."

"What has she been into?" he asked Elizabeth.

"Only a little rum."

"You'd better take her below and put her to bed."

"I'm not going anywhere. Tim and I are going to do some jigging."

"Your father would love to catch a sight of that!"

A mutilated hand punched out of the mist. Tim Healy was seized by the neck, and as the fog peeled away, a face hung behind the hand, outraged and intense. Doctor Jones snapped the boy back and forth, grabbing at the red rag tied around Tim's forehead. Another ferocious shake. A glimpse of Tim's popping eyes, and then he shook himself loose and dived off into the fog, the cook raving at his heels. Screams. Thumps. Silence. A wild shriek from overhead. Tim's head appeared briefly at the topgallant yardarm, howling for help and mercy.

27

It was Jock who spun himself up into the rigging with spidery grace, coaxed Timothy Healy down from the topmast, persuaded him to give back Doctor Jones's red amulet, and calmed them both down. The cook waved his mangled hands, and said he'd awakened to find the cloth missing from his head, a thing as terrible as being scalped in his sleep. Tim Healy couldn't remember when or why he'd done it. Rum had erased a full day of his life, until he'd found himself nesting like a seabird high over the ocean while Doctor Jones waited below to stick him with a knife. The experience was terrifying enough to persuade him to hand over the gallon jug, and what remained in it, to his berthmates. It was safer, he later told Cathleen, to be sober and safe, than drunken and dead. And with that remark Tim Healy picked up his worrying again as easily as a dropped stocking.

Cathleen never knew for sure whether the rum cured her cold or not. She was too sick to care about anything, and the jolting dose she had taken scrambled her tongue, muddled her thoughts, and clamped on a headache that lasted for days. The measles that appeared on her face were anticlimactic, hardly worth bothering about. Cholera, shipwreck, burial at sea were things she could face more easily than a morning after drinking rum. But even worse than the combined effects of the alcohol and the measles was the dim memory of telling Jock Riordan to go climb a rope, and the depression that followed.

She lay in the berth in the passenger cabin, and discovered that all vitality, hope, and humor had ebbed away and that she no longer cared much about anything around her, or anything that might lie ahead. Now she understood why some people died so easily, and why others, like Bartley, did not. It was a loss of curiosity about life that killed the spirit quickly. She felt that loss within herself. The strain of all that had happened had been too great. Her trouble had always been that she cared too much. Jock, for instance. All that spilled emotion had left her empty. Now she only wanted for Elizabeth to leave her alone, to stop talking at her, to leave her becalmed, like a brig without wind, in the privacy of this strange indifference.

"The cold is so intense on deck that nobody can stand it for more than a few minutes at a time," Elizabeth told her, coming into the cabin from a walk on the quarterdeck and looking as if she'd enjoyed it. "There are fishing fleets out there. I saw more than a hundred and fifty sloops anchored along the Banks to catch the cod."

Cathleen wasn't interested in the cold or the cod. But Elizabeth, who had once had difficulty deciding what dress to put on in the morning, crackled about the cabin, straightening Cathleen's berth, combing her hair, bullying Thomas into bringing oatmeal and hot drinks at all hours for her to make faces at. "Shall I get a message to Jock, that you're sick with the measles? I imagine he's worried at not seeing you."

"No, let him think I'm a reprobate. I don't care."

"But you *did* care."

"Love's a peculiar fever, and I'm thankful I'm over it."
And Cathleen put her head under the pillow.

Daily Elizabeth plunged into the squalor of steerage to bring back news of the O'Faoláins. Bartley was getting stronger and noisier every minute, and Mrs. Rourke was already complaining about him again. Mrs. Russell was more cantankerous than ever since she'd been deprived of the shoes and the shirts she'd been expecting for Mortimer. Mary Kate was smiling now, in spite of the terrible smell. There were still the daily burials. "They've run out of old sail to wrap the bodies in. Imagine, Cathleen, people dropped overboard in meal sacks. It's dreadful. No prayers or ceremony at all, sometimes nobody left to mourn, or care. But I care. I've raved at the captain so many times that he runs when he sees me. But he's finally partitioned off the sick from the well, and perhaps that will help slow the contagion. Now if he'll only send sailors below to clean up the mess. It's ankle-deep in filth."

Every night in a tight, indignant script, Elizabeth recorded what had passed during the day. The pages of her journal were crammed with details about the brig: the dimensions of the steerage, the quantity and quality of the ship's rations, the water supply, the kinds of diseases, the number of deaths. She was full of plans and energy, and when Cathleen wanted to escape into sleep, she kept her awake by reading to her.

"Not essays or poetry anymore. There's a time and a place for those, and it isn't here or now. I'll read about revolutions instead. They're full of dreams and violence, better for you than a tonic."

Cathleen, through no wish of her own, but only to

please Elizabeth Arnold, listened to revolutions, ate and drank, sat up in bed, and at last climbed out of it.

Fogbound, creaking and rocking, the *Fair Western Lady* traveled slowly past the coast of Cape Breton, wove a course through the field ice, and finally entered the strait between Cape North and Cape Ray. "Ice ahead" was shouted again and again as the brig steered a cautious path through the scattered puzzle of the floes. Elizabeth was on deck to watch and report the progress back to Cathleen. St. Paul Island was a graveyard, she said, the rocky shores strewn with the splintered bones of many sailing ships that had been carried beyond their reckoning. At last they were safely past, into the Gulf of St. Lawrence and the final phase of the voyage. There was a great fishing party and mackerel were hauled up in large numbers.

"Thank God for that," Elizabeth said. "Many of the emigrants are out of food. If only the water were fresh here, instead of salty. Some have drunk it anyway and become very ill."

"I want to see my family."

"And they want to see you; they've all been so worried. So you must come up on deck. Besides, we're approaching the Bird Islands, and it's really quite a sight. Come on, put on one of my shawls over your own, and wrap up warmly. It's still very cold."

28

For the first time in many days Cathleen stood in the clean air, drawing deep breaths. She shivered, in spite of the many layers of wool wrapped around her body. The Bird Islands were low ledges of rock; they swarmed and heaved and fluttered with thousands of gannets, birds large as geese, with white wings tipped in black. As she watched their constant motion and heard their ringing cries Cathleen felt as if she were slowly awakening on the other side of a long, dark night.

"Look," Elizabeth said. "Your father has just carried Bartley up from below."

Cathleen rushed to see them, to throw her arms around them both and tell them, yes, she was fine again, only a little shaky at the knees. She could see that her father was pleased to see her, to know that she was alright. Bartley was only a splinter of himself, but as busy as ever, flapping his arms crazily at the gannets as he talked, and full of information about Pygmies. "Wish I could see one. Only as tall as me they are, and wear skirts made of leaves."

"You can tell me all about them later," Cathleen said. "Right now I'm going to see Mother and Mary Kate."

On her way down the ladder she heard her name called.

"There you are, girl! Oh, but I've missed you."

"Irish girls are plentiful," she said to Jock. "If you miss one, there'll be another along soon enough." And she ducked down the hatchway.

Anticosti was treacherous, surrounded by sunken reefs, and they had just safely passed it when Captain Greeley appeared on the quarterdeck and fired off the old blunderbuss.

"It's only a signal," the second mate soothingly told Elizabeth. "Soon a pilot will come and guide us in."

"That's a relief." She smiled at him. "I thought for a moment that he meant to take a shot at me."

They were still two hundred miles from Quebec. As the brig tacked throughout the day, the emigrants who were still able to walk on deck glimpsed both sides of the great St. Lawrence. The scenery was vast and overpowering, continuously changing. High green shoulders of mountains, wide bays, thick pine forests. Along the shorelines mist dissolved like smoke, exposing capes, valleys, and ravines. Only Timothy Healy was depressed, as he huddled at Liddy Dillon's heels. "I dreamed last night that this brig caught fire, and all of us burned like biscuits. There's many have dreamed of disaster and later found it come to pass."

"Oh, my timbers, I should hope not," Liddy said, with a flash of her old humor. "For I had a nightmare myself, that we were married, Tim, with a lot of morbid children all in black rags, like a flock of scarecrows."

A schooner drew up alongside the brig, and the pilot came on board. He was a great block of a man, roughly finished and crudely colored, and he spoke a garbled French and English that nobody could fully understand.

He handed the captain the quarantine regulations, and then, with a wild holler, scattered a handful of maple sugar candy among the children. Cathleen scrambled with the pack, and captured a piece for Bartley. "But save a taste for Mary Kate."

"She hasn't any teeth," he said, and swallowed it all.

A cask of sweet water was brought on board from the schooner. The emigrants leaned forward, watched as the keg was uncorked and passed hand to hand among the crew. The sailors drank deeply, gasped, wiped their wet mouths with the backs of their hands, and drank again. The captain poured a cup, and with a sardonic smile offered it to Elizabeth.

"If the Irish can't have fresh water, then why should I?" she told him, and refused it.

For several days the pilot guided them deeper into the gulf, past hills, coves, settlements of little whitewashed cottages, whose red roofs and yellow doors reminded Cathleen of the sketches of a happy child. At night a fantasy of northern lights surged overhead.

Grosse Isle lay just ahead. As they came toward it, under a haze of warm July sunshine, the captain ordered the sailors below to begin the purification of the brig. The *Fair Western Lady* moved lightly among dozens of other vessels until it dropped anchor at last and hoisted its ensign at the peak as a signal for the inspection physician to come on board.

29

"Purified!" Liam O'Faoláin spat out the words between his teeth. He paced the deck, holding Mary Kate bundled against his chest. "They'll never get the stink out of this brig, not unless they burn her."

"Look! The Isle of Pestilence," the Portuguese seaman whispered dramatically. In the distance lay Grosse Isle, picturesque in the sunlight. The emigrants saw a fort, a chapel, an innocent small village and its wharf. "The Isle of Death!" The Portuguese flumed tobacco juice upon the deck and turned away in disgust.

"Thirty-three miles from Quebec," Mr. O'Faoláin went on, not caring who heard him, "and *now* the brig must be cleaned for inspection. If we'd had regular inspections weeks ago there would be more of us alive today. It's criminal, his neglect, criminal."

Captain Greeley ignored him. Sailors moved up and down through the open hatchways, dragging out straw mattresses and throwing them overboard.

"And what will we sleep on tonight?" Mrs. Roohan fiercely tugged at one end of her mattress as one of the young apprentices pulled on the other.

"Captain says fresh straw will be sent out from the island."

"Indeed! Then I'll wait until it gets here before I give up my bed."

The seaman gave a final wrench, grabbed up the mattress, and tossed it over the side. "Captain's orders, ma'am."

The passengers had been out of bed since dawn. The brig rocked with activity. Unless the vessel was scrubbed, whitewashed, and certified pure, it would not be allowed to complete the voyage. The Irish had been ordered to throw every scrap of rubbish overboard, to wash and dress themselves in their best and cleanest clothing. Soon the physician would arrive to inspect them, and the sick would be sent into quarantine on the island. The healthy, Captain Greeley assured them, would be transferred to a steamer and immediately sent on to Quebec.

Cathleen went below to help her parents. Their berth was already orderly, the mattress destroyed, their luggage packed and tied with cord. Sailors scooped up armloads of belongings in their hurry to clean out the mess, and emigrants fought to reclaim them. Rags, moldy provisions, discarded clothing, and broken crockery were heaped into the center aisle. Cathleen saw something that looked familiar and worked it loose. It was a large fragment of the painted chamber pot Aunt Wig had given them. If Aunt Wig could see them now she would weep for them, Cathleen thought. Someday she would write and tell her about the voyage, but it would be a long time before she could put into words what the Irish had been through. Yet there were good things to remember, too. Things to make Aunt Wig laugh, and herself in the years to come.

Straw mattresses split, scattering their stuffing from one end of steerage to another. Bartley stuck on a wig and a beard, hobbled and quavered like an old man, got in everyone's way, and was sent up on deck.

At noon there was a shout that the doctor had arrived. An exhausted-looking man with a drooping moustache, he was brief and businesslike. "Is there sickness on board?"

The captain admitted there was some.

"Its nature?"

"Mostly the fever. And cholera. Measles, too. Dysentery, of course."

"How many deaths, sir?"

Captain Greeley held out his dry, white hands hopelessly. "I don't have that information yet, doctor. There's been no time for statistics."

"Forty." Liam O'Faoláin spoke out strongly. "Forty dead, doctor. All Irish."

"And how many ill at present?"

Again the captain shrugged. "If you'd like to step below and see for yourself . . ."

"Fifteen confined to their berths in serious condition," said Mr. O'Faoláin. "They've knocked the beds out from under the rest of us."

The doctor scribbled information on his official forms, then went between decks with the captain. After a short time he returned and handed over a sheaf of papers. "Fill these in. I'll be back to pick them up in a day or two." He was over the side, and soon his dory was seen moving on to another vessel anchored nearby.

"A day or two, is it!" Mrs. Roohan clamped her arms across her chest. "And our mattresses gone. All of us, fools that we are, dressed in our best and nowhere to go.

A hospital in sight, but not a drop of medicine for our sick. A river inches away, and not a bit of it fit to drink. What other tortures do you have in store for us, Captain?"

Late in the afternoon two priests arrived in a dory and asked permission to come on board. One of them was very old, with trembling hands and lips, and eyes that leaked slow tears. His assistant was young and brisk, and spoke only French.

"Ask if they'll baptize Mary Kate," Mrs. O'Faoláin whispered to her husband. "I've been terrified all this while that something would happen to her before she received the Holy Sacrament. Ask, Liam, before they go away."

"Me, too," Bartley said. "If Mary Kate gets to be baptized, so do I."

Cathleen hauled him back as he took off after the skirts of the priests. "You've been done already."

"I don't remember it."

"Well, I remember it very well. You screeched as if Father McConaghy planned to boil you, not bless you."

The priests stayed until twilight, giving the last rites to the dying and hearing confessions. The young couple who had become engaged on the Atlantic asked urgently to be married, as a child was already on the way. Mary Kate, yawning and serene, was sprinkled with holy water, watched jealously by Bartley, who wanted to be a part of the ceremony. Fever patients moaned, and as the priests prepared to leave, white-haired old Mr. Gogarty struggled and cursed in his berth, threatening to kill them both.

The ship's lanterns gleamed, cat's eyes in the soft, black body of the summer night.

"You could go ahead on the first steamer tomorrow," Cathleen said. "Cabin passengers don't need to go through regular inspection."

"No, I'm staying to see what happens," Elizabeth insisted. "It's important that I know."

"But we have no idea how long we'll be stuck here."

"At least I have a bed. What about the others, lying on bare boards below?"

"Thank God the weather's warm, not wet."

"I've been thinking that perhaps you'd like to travel with me to my father's place. I'd like that so much. We could study together . . . I'd teach you anything you like. Even Greek, if you'd fancy it."

Cathleen laughed. "I'm not sure how handy that would be in the Canadian wilderness." She was surprised and pleased and not sure how she should answer.

"It's not that I'm afraid to go on alone. My father's a stranger, but he's always been a stranger. It's because we're such good friends. And it might be a help to your family."

Cathleen liked and admired Elizabeth Arnold, who had opened windows for her that would soon be shut again. They had been good for each other. It would be hard to be permanently separated from her family. But it was true that her wages might make the farm possible sooner. Maybe her father would even be relieved to have her off his hands and earning her own keep.

"Will you consider it?"

"Yes, I'll consider it."

30

Restless and anxious, the emigrants awaited the physician's return. In final desperation, many of them had drunk water from the harbor; it had made them sick, and they were afraid they would be put into quarantine. They tried to stay on their feet, to freshen their wrinkled clothing, to look healthy and cheerful and neat, but it was a poor showing.

One of the vessels had an ensign hung at half-mast, and Liddy Dillon came to tell Cathleen that the brig was the *Fitzroy* out of Cork. "Remember when we spoke her at sea? I've heard that most of her passengers are dead of cholera, and that the captain himself is to be buried today at Grosse Isle."

Cathleen found she was almost numb to such reports. "Won't you be glad when inspection is over and we're finally on our way? Will you be alright, Liddy?"

"Lord, yes. I'll find employment soon enough at Hambleton, I'm sure of that."

"When you look back on all of this—" Cathleen tried to sort out the right words from the wrong ones—"I hope you'll remember me as a friend. You were good to me, I know I'll remember that."

"Not always, I wasn't." Liddy's damaged face tightened. "And I don't want to look back on any of this, ever. I did what I had to do to get here, but that debt is paid.

And I still believe it's better to be a living sinner than a buried saint, don't you?" She laughed outright, and tucked her arm through Cathleen's. "Say, did you notice the steamer that left the harbor this morning with people dancing on deck, fiddle and all? Wasn't it a grand sight to see? Do you suppose we could do the same on our way to Quebec?"

At last the doctor's boat was sighted, and in minutes he was on board, collecting the forms and papers he had left with Captain Greeley.

"How many are ill today, Captain?"

"Two more down with cholera. That makes seventeen in serious condition."

"We can't take them all. Have eight of the worst ready to leave in an hour, and the rest will have to wait their turn. But it's never long, I guarantee that. Twenty-five hundred are confined in hospital already, but beds empty out so fast we can't keep enough coffins on hand."

Eight of the sick were brought from below and placed on the deck. Some of the emigrants tried to shelter the patients from the bright sunlight, while others drew away, afraid of contamination. As Jock Riordan and one of the apprentices carried up the last one, Cathleen knelt and folded part of a quilt under the woman's head.

"Do you know her?" Jock asked.

"Ah, yes. It's Mrs. Russell."

He spoke quietly. "What will become of her children, I wonder. They're sitting all in a row down below, poor little devils, looking as if they've forgotten how to breathe."

"She's dying?"

"Yes, she's dying."

Cathleen bent over Mrs. Russell and looked into her face. It was a ghastly and determined mask, the mouth clamped shut, the hard features still twisted and awry. Cathleen spoke her name. The eyes opened and stared.

"Mrs. Russell? Was someone to meet you in Quebec?" She tried again, not knowing what it was she must say. "Do you have relatives in Canada? Someone who might help care for the children?"

A negative shake of the head. The eyes were pale, flat, emptied of all dreams. Then Mrs. Russell made a curious gesture, a pushing, defeated motion of her hand. It was as if she finally rejected all hope, and life itself, with its hardships, indignities, and suffering.

Urgently Cathleen asked, "What can I do for you?"

The words came distinctly, full of fury. "Go and be damned."

Jock's hand touched down upon Cathleen's hair, and then the side of her cheek as she crouched over the body. "Poor soul, she's gone," he said.

Cathleen looked up at him. "Oh, if you'd seen the way she fought and scrapped and clawed her way along to get here. I only wish she'd made it! I wish she had!"

The sailors prepared to lower the longboat. Suddenly the emigrants realized what was about to happen, and a crescendo of cries and shrieks went up as sick children were taken from their distracted parents, husbands from wives, dying parents from healthy children. A man recently recovered from ship fever rushed up to Captain Greeley. "You can't take my wife. What will happen to Sara when she recovers and finds herself all alone, with no money to pay for a passage to Quebec? How will she find me again? I can't let her go. I must go with her."

The first mate took hold of him and struggled with him as his wife was removed to the longboat. Mrs. O'Faoláin put her arms around Mrs. Hoult, and the two women rocked back and forth for comfort as Johnny Hoult was placed with the others. "Seven years old, and to go all alone to that terrible place. He'll think we've abandoned him. Why can't I go with him?"

"Shhhh, oh, please, Mrs. Hoult. They'll make him well again, and then we'll all help you to get him back, wait and see. You shall have him back with you, I promise you that."

Cathleen gripped Jock's arm. "What will happen to these people if they're separated? How will they ever find each other again?"

"I don't know. I honestly don't know."

All day and into the evening the waking nightmare went on, until the last of the seventeen patients had been transferred to the island hopsital. The berths were broken up and thrown overboard, and the Irish forced to spend another night without mattresses. The hold had been scrubbed and purified, the last smudge of grime buried under a thick concealing coat of whitewash. Cathleen remembered what her father had said, and knew that he was right. The sad smell of poverty, disease, and death would never be wiped away from the *Fair Western Lady*. She remembered how it had been at the outset, the laughter and dancing as they sailed out of Dublin, a hundred and ten of them, buoyant with hope. Now, fewer than sixty were left. The voyage was almost over, but all the hardships of a strange northern land still lay ahead. They had survived so much. She wondered how much more they could endure.

31

The breeze blew up Mary Kate's fine ruffle of hair. Her small neck wobbled as she blinked against the dazzle of light upon the water.

"She'll remember none of this," said her mother.

"The rest of us will never forget it," Cathleen said. "Have you seen Father? There's something I must say to him."

"Mrs. O'Faoláin!" young Mrs. Rourke interrupted, her hands pushed into her plump hips. She blushed with anger. "That Bartley of yours, he's driving me to desperation."

"And what's he done now, Mrs. Rourke?"

"He's engaged in a spitting contest at present. I won't have it, Mrs. O'Faoláin, it's disgusting."

"I'll speak to him at once. Oh, and one thing, Mrs. Rourke, in case we shouldn't meet again."

"What's that?"

"I hope, when you have children of your own, that they'll be a joy and a comfort to you."

"I'll stand for no nonsense, I can promise you that. It's firmness, you see, and discipline, and a sound beating wherever it's required that make an obedient, good child. Some have a talent for motherhood, I've observed, and others do not. *Obedience,* Mrs. O'Faoláin, is what I shall expect and demand."

186

She flounced away, and Mrs. O'Faoláin whispered to Cathleen, "A woman who takes no pleasure in her children has frost on her soul. So let her live her lifetime in January, for all I care, but I pity her. I'd rather have you and Bartley and Mary Kate than any she's likely to prod along in the world. And Cathleen, you've grown up on me this voyage, turned into a fine young woman in the blink of an eye."

"I doubt if Father would ever agree with that."

"The trouble with you and Liam is that you're too much alike, too strong and outspoken. You'll be scrapping away until kingdom come. I'd be willing to bet on it. But in a way you're luckier than he is. You can see the foolish crooked side of life, and he only sees what's solemn and straight. It's hard to live with that, Cathleen. And you and Bartley, for all your nonsense, make it lighter for me."

Tim Healy stopped to tell them that the steamer would be by in the afternoon to pick up the passengers for Quebec, as soon as the brig had been given a clean bill of health.

"And what will you do when you get there?"

"They say employment is easy to find, Mrs. O'Faoláin. I'll find one trade or another. Perhaps, with the cholera so bad, thousands dead I hear, I'll go into coffin-making."

"Then I hope you make your fortune at it," Cathleen said.

"No, no . . . there's little chance of that. The winters are so fierce here, I've been told. I'm more likely to end up with chilblains than cash."

They had packed up the last of the books and put them in the trunk with the rest of Elizabeth's belongings.

"Have you spoken to your father yet?" she asked.

"Not yet. I'll find him now and do it."

Elizabeth picked up her journal and ran her fingers through the pages. "At least, for now, I feel I have some purpose. I'm going to write up this report, and direct it to the proper place—the House of Lords if I have my way. If I never do another useful thing in my whole life, perhaps some good will come of it, some changes and reforms. Perhaps someday people might read it and think this voyage was a fiction. But it really happened, didn't it, Cathleen?"

"Yes, just as you've written it. It's a fine thing you've done, an important and necessary thing, and I'm proud of you."

Bartley's head popped in at the cabin door. "Father says we're to be inspected now."

"And how's Mary Kate?" Elizabeth teased him.

"I still don't like that baby." Bartley screwed up his face.

"You will one day."

"No, I won't. Cathleen's the one I like."

"Would you mind very much if your sister traveled on with me?"

"Yes, I'd mind. And anyway she can't—she's ours." Then he remembered. "Look what Jock gave to me! Said I could keep it." He put the round hat with streamers on his head, and his face almost disappeared under it.

"So he does keep his promises," Cathleen said.

"He's been wanting to speak to you, so I told him you were here, and he asked if you'd see him now."

Elizabeth said, "Send him in quickly, Bartley, before the captain sees. You and I will go up on deck together and wait for your sister."

They were out of the cabin and gone. Cathleen stood in the middle of the tiny room, hearing Harvey whistle and sing in the captain's quarters. Then there was Jock, shirt rolled up to the elbows, the mermaid swimming blithely down his arm.

"Well!"

"Well?"

"The steamer is ready to take you on, as soon as inspection is over."

"Yes," she said, "we've heard."

"That's fine . . ."

"So it's farewell, Jock." She said it coolly, thinking how worldly she sounded. Then she knew that she must tell him her feelings before it was too late. Better to spend the words now than to hoard them inside, of no use to anyone. That's what she'd always done, there was no changing it. She took his hands and said, "Oh, but I'm going to miss you, Jock. I'll think of you always and miss you forever, and I'm full of love for you, I am!"

"You couldn't let *me* say it first off, could you!"

"Is that why you've come?" Incredulous, she stared at him. "And here I was thinking that if I waited for you to say it I'd be too old and deaf to hear it." He laughed at that and she said, "Then what does it matter who says it first, as long as it's said?"

"Now *listen*." He was suddenly serious. "I'm not as handy with the words as you, nor as loud, either, nor as quick to come to grips with something as unexpected and confusing as love. I feel the same about you as you do about me, only quieter, that's all, and bewildered as to how all of this came about . . . no, let me finish . . . but I do know you're a wonderful bit of luck that's come into my life."

"We just met up at the wrong time, didn't we?"

"No, it was the right time. No matter where I go I'll have you to think on and I'll remember the night of the corposant and how it was the very best night of my life," he said. "But I'll be back someday for another look at you."

"And how will you find me?"

His quick smile. "Do you think I'll have a moment's trouble finding *you*? Canada's a grand big country for sure, but I'll just listen for the ruckus and there you'll be, right in the middle of it."

"It had better be sooner than someday, Jock, or I'll set out after you myself."

He laughed and said that to be on the safe side they would write letters just like any courting couple. He held her and touched her hair and she knew it was really farewell, that the long passage was ended. Both of them had other places to go, other things to do. Then he saw her eyes. "Don't cry now. Or say anything at all. Give me a kiss to remember you by, and another one after that. Cathleen . . . Cathleen O'Faoláin, what a lovely girl you are!"

The voyage had begun with a medical inspection. Soon it would end with one. Cathleen, standing with her father, discovered how much taller she had grown.

"Miss Arnold wants me to go with her as a companion to her father's place in Peterborough County. I'll send my wages on to you; it will be a help when you buy land for the farm." She waited. "Did you hear what I said, Father?"

"Your mother won't allow it."

"But you could persuade her it's the thing for me to do."

"No."

"I've always been a care and a trouble to you, there's no pretending otherwise."

He looked down at her. "Did you not hear me the first time, young woman? I said *no.*"

She flared up. "You've a fine chance to have me off your hands for good. You might give me a reason!"

"We need you," he said. "And that's the end of it."

He would never say the words she most wanted to hear, and yet what he had said was good enough. It would do.

The doctor's tired face, his intelligent, quick eyes, words she had heard once before. "Name and age? Are you well? Hold out your tongue. Alright."

About the Author

Norah A. Perez was born in Haileybury, Ontario, and graduated from St. Lawrence University in Canton, New York. She is the daughter of Leslie McFarlane, who wrote the first twenty volumes of the original Hardy Boys series. The author of several magazine pieces, television adaptations, and a novel for young people, Ms. Perez wrote *The Passage* in an attempt to recreate for herself the sea voyage taken by her Irish ancestors to Canada. She lives with her husband and three sons in Youngstown, New York.